STEPHEN'S LANDING

Stephen's Landing

A novel

by

GREGORY VINCENT ST. THOMASINO

Adelaide Books
New York / Lisbon
2020

STEPHEN'S LANDING
A novel
By Gregory Vincent St. Thomasino

Cover design © 2020 Adelaide Books
Cover art by Carol St. Thomasino

Published by Adelaide Books, New York / Lisbon
adelaidebooks.org

Editor-in-Chief
Stevan V. Nikolic

For any information, please address Adelaide Books
at info@adelaidebooks.org

or write to:

Adelaide Books
244 Fifth Ave. Suite D27
New York, NY, 10001

ISBN: 978-1-953510-95-2

Printed in the United States of America

for Cubby

I have an old-ethnic-New York face. I've seen my face in photographs in yellowed magazines in used-book shops. Here I am, Times Square, New Year's Eve, 1941. And here, I'm skating, the skating rink at Rockefeller Center. And here I am at Herald Square at Christmas time, the sidewalk outside Macy's. I'm the child reaching for the woman's hand.

My face is too serious. I am too young to be of such serious face. This fact notwithstanding, it is said my stare can wreck stone upon a nemesis. This is the asylum of mirrors.

Oh, so many children toddle by, I can't begin to count them all.

I said that in another life. Another time. Another age. Tonight,

The sulfurous nights. The air becomes increasingly pernicious.
And as streetlight so augments the gaseous poisons,
we are subject to nightly parades of ludicrous floats.

Outside, the smell of shit in the air. Wailing children spelling their frustration. Ugly mothers botching their discipline. And unlucky fathers without money. The dollar is their god. The lottery, their miracle. Or else, *Release us, O Mother of God.* Death, the great atonement.

History is dyspeptic. We are the age of culminations. The culmination of the worship of money, of urban luxury, of artificiality and vice. What exquisite hallucination. My face, New York City, the smell of shit in the air.

And after loving, we say nothing. There is no sign of affection. Only our sounds, the bodies relaxing. Side by side we lay, withdrawn into our helplessnesses.

—Why such pessimism? she asks.

—Pessimism? Or is it, clairvoyance?

—Converge. Again she starts it. Forces do, they must or be dispersed. *Politics. Dictatorships. Religious authoritarians. Fanaticals. Terror.* What solution? Angels of God coupled with *Uzi* submachine guns?

It was Lydia's manner of launching her words. Catapulting finality.

—You do not participate! she sallies. Not beyond lending us your presence.

I began a list of torture devices.

Boot

Ducking stool

Branks

—When I hold you I am solacing a child. A child who sculpts his thoughts into beauty, yet so pliant are these thoughts, he cannot be done with them.

Rack and candle

—I'm going, Stephen. I didn't plan to spend the night.

I can observe her dressing from my pillow. I am susceptible only to her hair.

Wheat blond

—You were not here tonight, Stephen.

Clinical blond

—I'll call. Maybe. After classes. If I have the time. I have office hours.

Strappado
Thumbscrew
Stiletto heels

—Come on, Stephen. Pull yourself out of it, will ya? I'm depressed enough as it is.

Wheel
Engine Co. No. 44 lipstick

The history of the City of New York can be recorded on a postage stamp.

$

I will not leave my bed today. Rather, I'll sleep in. I'll dream of pigs and pork and bacon and how these are prepared in Chinese restaurants, and when she calls I'll say I've prepared a sumptuous feast.
There's so much to digest!

I cannot see the stars. I cannot trace the constellations. What was I? Six? Seven? Pointing to the Little Dipper. Ursa Minor, the baby bear. Ursa Major, the daddy bear. They were Draco, whose snout is breathing flame, and Hercules, bursting through a chain. But I cannot see the stars! For skyscrapers, skyscrapers and scattered light! Our unhallowed halo. Our dross. Scattered light! It is the obfuscation of Heaven. A darkening.

We have interpreted away all the gnosis!

The ruler, striking the table, makes happen the smack. I wonder. *Have I taken my smacks for granted?*

Well, yes. And could you contain them smacks in a vessel of some kind, say, in your memory, why you would not need to speak at all, you would simply unloose a smack upon demand—a little smack as accords, say, a child, or a big smack as accords, say, an adult, and you might save the greatest smack for a thief or for your landlord, while the sweetish smacks can go to Lydia's behind. Well, yes. And she will call you Happy!

Mommy's always giving me kisses.

Mommy, or mammy, from mammary, meaning breast.

I mean with her lips!

Of course you do. So when a child cries for mommy, is he not in fact crying for a breast? It's only natural, then, that a child's first words be mommy.

Well, yes. But what if the child learns daddy first? Does that, then, mean that child will develop a complex? I mean, what if the mother dies in labor? What if the father alone raises the child? What if the wet nurse remains a stranger? Or maybe there was no wet nurse at all! What if the child should mature never knowing the oh! heavenly pacification of a nipple in the mouth? Will that child grow up to be a breast man? Chances are that man will behinds adore.

Butcher. The he-goat. Brisket. Flank. Rump. Loin. Fore- and hindshank. Chuck. Chop. Rib. Fillet. She's rather beefy in those early photographs. Now she's rather fit. Rather fit, I'd say. Her behind is really two small melons.

I am under surveillance. The strongest link in their chain of command is an Hispanic woman, one Marie X.

Damn those low branches. Ave Marie. And that infernal mule, bouncing me like some Naples bride. Ave Marie. I was seeing to the blankets, they were never enough. And my infernal piles! Ave Marie. Take your eyes off the road for one second, and ahi!

Passions and objects and objects of passion, succor and love.

My, my, Heloïse, I've done things absentmindedly. Join the curtain, next the door. Let us forego talk of lecher and whore. Let us rejoice in the divinity of the soul. For friendship is a sacred thing, of sacred things to speak after loving, or great catastrophe.

Her art had formed appeal to his intellect. Her beauty, to his spirit. He thought her symbolic of tragedy, next joyful, of all joy and triumph she seemed.

We by heavens parted be. Our twin nostalgia, rascality.

A constellation.

In a month or so I'll grow bedsores. What will she say to that?

—Let me smooth some elbows on your cream. *Feel better?*

—Delightful. *Some here?*

—I see. . . .

—And my shoulder blades.

—I see. Why don't I just give you a rub? So tell me what you did today.

—Well, after long deliberation the gods have seen fit to ratify my proposition. We'll be raising the new constellation on the evening of the fifteenth.

—You don't say. Congratulations.

—Draco's out of town 'til the thirteenth, Hercules enters the clinic on the seventeenth. The most crucial obstacle, *filling those two vacant spaces,* was finally hurdled late last Saturday when the Big Man made a show and came 'round to granting us a couple stars.

—Quite an accomplishment.

—I'd say. He won long applause. And then you know, the entire chamber turned 'round and applauded *me. The Big Man too!* Although He didn't stand. You know I have to admit I was a bit choked up. Then Cepheus tapped me on the shoulder, and guess what? Cassiopeia kissed me on the cheek! Hercules invited me out for a drink, but I declined. *You know what happened the last time we went out drinking two-o'clock in the morning.*

—A national disgrace!

—I'd say. I got off easy. *The press has yet to forgive Herc.*

—Do you suppose those women'll ever get their lives back in order?

—Beats me.

"The Whale"

It lived downstairs, in the Men's room, at the old Brunswick alleys where my league used to bowl. Some boys, my age—twelve or thirteen, probably a little older—lured me down there and instructed me on how to coax it from its slumbers. You had to stand on a particular spot and jump up a bit to catch hold of this metal bar that was a part of the stalls. Then, dangling for an instant, you reached for the hot-air blower and pushed its *On* button.

This simultaneous action—of holding to the bar whilst engaging the blower button—resulted, more often than not, in the delivery of an electrical shock. And for an instant you're made helpless, dangling there like an idiot while the boys gathered 'round you have a fit.

And so, my fellow electricians, I leave you with this thought, but more than a thought, really, a fact. In the words of the great Watschandis, who dig a hole and dance around it with their spears held in front to simulate an erect penis, Not a pit, not a pit, but a cunt!

There is an essay, over a century old, by one Dr. S.J. Holmes in which it is reasoned the role of sex in the evolution of the mind. Here one finds compared the elaborate wooing of male birds—their mating call, that is—with the articulate language of man in such summation as the function of the voice in the vertebrates is primarily to serve as a sex call. Granting this, the most eloquent of speakers ought to be among the most alluring—sexually winning, that is—and conversely, the sexually alluring ought to be found among the vocally eloquent. Now on the whole, this is untrue. Although there are exceptions. Some choice exceptions can be found at *the opera. . . .*

* phase in the Wagner

Homeless—incoherent for the most part, and ravenous—inhabit the wasteways beneath Grand Central Terminal. Babes are torn from nursing arms and devoured unspitted less salt, white pepper, rosemary, thyme, secret Cajun blackening spices, extra virgin olive oil, hot mustard—*from those little plastic packets that you can't let go of*—vinegar and bay leaf—*pigs' feet in a bottle, or, how many pickled pigs' feet are in fact pickled baby parts?*

Will charity restore their faith in the upper classes?
It all boils down to human sacrifice.

Abraham and Isaac.
The Big Man and the Little Big Man.
How many angels of God coupled with *Uzi*
submachine guns.

Someday, somehow, *but certainly!* Archaeologists—*speaking what tongue?*—will uncover miscellaneous journals and synthesize by terrible degrees the exquisite hallucination we are living in.

*big crescendo on the Wagner, then *poof*

"Der Fall Stephen"

Route 27 stretches E. and W. Along its southern wayside lies a waste of sandy lot jostled through with Queen Anne's Lace. A tall wrought-iron railing marks a boundary for the Lutheran cemetery which keeps to the road for a quarter-mile. The morning traffic comes and goes infrequently then towards noon the road is packed with vehicles. When the weather is fair and the sand is dry, the earth-warmed air reflects the sky so as to be a rippling silver ocean. This causes the vehicles to pause. The drivers exit their cabs, raise a palm to their foreheads and wonder how real it is, then drive on into it.

In the cemetery the stones are mossed and forgotten. The rails are chapped and peeling.

Beyond the farthermost boundary is a schoolhouse. Through its tall, trim windows begabled with broken pediments a class of kindergartners is joining a circle to play an exercise. One child is refusing to join in. The teacher is scolding him. She cites his failed attempts at penmanship. She leads him to a chair beside a window.

It *is* an opera. A little opera. *Opera buffa,* that child, I. A bit too apprehensive for his own well-being, own sanity, own couth. Striking out at the adults less all restraint. Brazen and skeptical, and probably obnoxious. *Rehearsing my response?* I couldn't help myself, I didn't even have to think about it. *It just came to me!* Who figured they would hold a grudge? What sort of adult retaliates upon a child? I was writing G *hyphen* d, as the teacher had us do. Who knew from Christian and Jew? Children aren't bigots, 'cept adults make them so. And that clumsy little man, the one who owned the candy store, the one whose accent we could not make out, the one who sold us the cigarettes and warned us with a fist not to read the dirty paperbacks. I said, *you ought to be open on Saturdays and closed on Sunday, like everybody else.* Who knew what the tattoo meant? Even among philosophers, I have not found philosophers but Christians and Jews. Access and control, that's what you're all about. *You. The priests. The police.* Sucking fat from a Chinese rib, dipping the rib into that little plastic cup of duck sauce, and then one quick dip into that little plastic cup of yellow mustard. What's in that duck sauce, anyway? *Minced foetus, honey and salt?* Are you a feminist? I love you. Spy on me. Murder me. Choke me. I can't tolerate you. What do you suggest? So compressed. *So on.* This proves the utmost quandary. For a qualitatively greater apprehension admits a greater cross withal its greater joy. Self-administered contrition. Redemptive thought—a virtue yet to be bested. For redemptive thought, if it is to effect its purpose, if it is to heal, to amend, to rectify, naturally requires—*requires what?* In no wise but by altering perspective, grasping this station now occupied as far removed from that of my childhood. Time alone cannot suffice, cannot provide a distance wherefrom reparations occur. *Repent!* Flying is just so much skillful falling. The psychology, left to itself, naturally sinks. All things that sink must disperse. *Amen*

"Stephen's Lake"

At their feet, traces of a path, slabs of slate long fractured into bits. *See that one, Stephen? Yes,* pointing to a spread of wild roses. *It's a garter, I know 'cause as a child one slid under my covers.* Carpeted, then, by bristle leaf, dusty cone, pressed by days, the lakeside seemed skirted in fur. And how her hair kept its brilliant *red,* despite cumulative clouds, mining the sunlight. The lake the color of the pine tar. The landing, that of the trunks. And as he aimed his eye for what awaited them, she took him with an embrace. He saw into her eyes to welcome what he knew would be their first confiding. She threw back her hair, eyes pitched at gray zenith, a tear streaking her temple. He kissed her neck and felt his cheek toward her tear, it was warm and soft and inside him. The lake reflected nothing. The landing throbbed, imparting cadence to the lake. She passed into that subtle surface, where they kissed, eyes pressing closed, as the water swirled and eddied, as dim circularities arose beneath to pillow their embrace letting fathom after fathom pass as the lake rose from its basin, rose above its shore, above the reaching pine to where it hovered among clouds. A warm, sunny twilight filled the basin. Clasping hands, both gathered into ken inhabitants long drawn from an initial berth. Wrecked oars. Gone tools. Gnarl and clenching bough once gasping for air. Now petrified trunk. Now petrified limb stump. The water swirled and eddied, thrusting them afloat. Rain burst down upon them. They held, treading, seeing all in wiling disarray.

The first college I attended was a small private two-year music school on the southern fork of Long Island. It was here that I learned piano and how to read and write music. *Of all the required courses I disliked solfeggio the most as my voice consistently refused to perform publicly thus causing myself, my instructor and my classmates, repeated disconcertion.* In sum, my study of music proved only privately rewarding. Accomplished musicianship was not, it now appears, my primary motivation. I did however gain the possession of a certain pleasurable memory as regards my English Literature instructor. She proposed I train my efforts to the *written* word.

Lydia was plain in that widely imitated Connecticut sense of plain. Comfortable moccasin loafers, blue candy stripes, Van Doren's *country wife* with straight blond hair to just above the collar in the neat appearance of a town girl. She drove to school in a white VW station wagon. The operative word, here, is white, as in no matter the make of the car, so long as it is white. Lydia led me to search for allegories in O'Connor and in Hawthorne. I wrote an exposition on "A Good Man Is Hard to Find" making a whole lot of mistrustful stuff out of Red Sammy's monkey and that chinaberry tree. I went so far as to mention Nostradamus. I wrote on Goodman Brown, comparing him alongside Faust. I made a great to-do over avoiding the Freudianesque and this, I suppose, was the edge to her interpreting my sensibilities as home grown.

Her schedule, it so turned out, was ordered so that our English Lit. session just happened to mark her final obligation of the school day. This coincidence facilitated our acquaintanceship, it brought us together in a somewhat extracurricular sense as we both eased into the habit of my accompanying her from the building. It was our routine that from the classroom she would next a quick stop into the department office, where she would signature the book, and from there we would continue for the parking lot. We would lean beside her car discussing, beyond the daily themes, my prospects for transfer to a traditional four-year institution. And sometimes, weather permitting, we would slip into the car and she would start the motor and turn on the windshield wipers.

Lydia must have sensed in my temperament some sort of emblematic or suggestive characteristic that had either gone unnoticed or had had a dissuasive influence upon my other instructors, both of this time and earlier. For she was being more than poetic when she told me, *You must not allow yourself to become discouraged. Your true mettle lies in perseverance.* I was not then prone nor indeed was I fit to interpret her remarks as anything like keen empathy or diagnosis, rather were they received as general if curiously stirring caution. Still, however, this was serious. *However should I become discouraged?*

According to Dr. Becker, man is an organism with two anuses, one of which has teeth. Had I become acquainted with Dr. Becker's summing up ten years ago I would today be guilty of a lot less speech. Which leads me to wonder, *if one can make eloquent one's speech, can one not, then, make eloquent one's shit?*

"How I Became Verbal Sadistic"

If you really want to hear about it, the first thing you'll probably want to know is what I ate and what TV shows I watched, how they plopped me in front of Bozo and filled my bottle with Pepsi, how I suckled ragged the corners of my pillows and bit off the noses of my teddy bears, how those teeth marks I left in Grandma's kitchen chair sent my father into a seizure, how he beat me, then, and how I wouldn't shit or speak to him for weeks, how my father flew for a commercial airline and could see me only once a week, and how I always managed to have diar-rhea on the nights he took me out, how he stopped bringing home his girlfriends, and all the sitters that I had, and how Aunt Gloria saw after us for a while at the beginning, and why I bit her, and how she said I was possessed and got this Catholic priest to talk to me, and how he said I was too headstrong to be possessed and started all that commotion about my welfare when I asked if he knew of any nuns who

were wet-nursing, and how they put me away and
I was forced to make confession and damn nearly
gagged on my Communion wafer.

—It's a sign! Auntie said.

How I showed up one morning at Newark Air-
port and nearly got my father fired, how he took me
up to Boston where he had an apartment and said
we were gonna start fresh, how the doctors said I was
sick, and how they gave me insulin, and how the
blonde nurse sat with me and showed me where with
the syringe, and how I never bit again but learned to
sublimate the urge by saying *fuck!*

And how the summers were so long. And probably, I suppose, because of all the disappointments. We built ourselves
a bungalow, just father and myself, atop this mountain where
the streams were packed with crayfish. The paths there were
ancient and strewn with shiny beads and arrowheads, all for
the collecting. On sunny days, and after rainfall, the bald rock
sparkled all its minerals. You could almost see the mushrooms
blooming. I found myself a friend with little Christopher, who
told me secrets, and I told him mine. *I'm happy to have you
for my friend,* he said. *And you for me,* I told him. We built a
tree house and carved our signs into the wood. Mine was an
arrowhead, his was a star. We slept inside a tepee at the bottom
of our tree and kept a fire going all night long. And then one
day, as I sat upon our roof handing nails and shingles to my
father, I noticed little Christopher coming up the road and I
was taken by the keenest intuition. Christopher, and I, and
my father and our house, and the nails and the hammer and
the shingle and the ladder and the ground and the sun and

the sky and the stream, and the crayfish, there. . . . We were all One. Us, all and everything was One. And Chris's shiny hair was a golden helmet, and in his arms he held a golden sword. I sprang to my feet, shouting, *Christopher! Up here!* My father was taken by surprise. He turned suddenly, to grab hold of me, and lost his balance. He fell from the roof and lost consciousness. And later that day, in the hospital bed, he died. And somehow, but leave it to the logic of adults, I was never to see Christopher again.

There is a space inside that house that I have never explored. It is the attic. And when he pulled that ladder down it brought with it such warm and succulent air. How I stood into that draft, as he climbed into the shadow, sustaining myself by his love.

Ice floe. The immaculate symmetry of snowflakes. How they hover, as though hesitant, sparkling diamond point, trailing varied color as they echo the light. A theory, recorded long before, how certain snow, lighting, makes friction in the air, and warmth.

—A child's theory, Stephen. But is it so?

—Does not this night's air welcome us, our open coats?

—Say will there be great snowfall this winter? I want to see this city halted under snow.

—I love a crippled city. *The sound of chains on snowplows.*

—*I see it!* Maybe the sky will clear and open up. And maybe, before we reach your building, *maybe we'll see stars. Stars make a miracle of snow.* I want to show you stars, Stephen. *Stars over snowy sidewalks!*

—I do not know too many stars. I look up and all I see are skyscrapers, skyscrapers and scattered light.

—I want to show you stars. I want to teach you how to read the constellations. You are the sort of person, Stephen, who no matter his age will always have his whole life ahead of him.

—It is but the illusion of poetry. *Which is why we need poetry!*

—It's something more than that. I know you, Stephen. It's this *prospective* thing you have. I'm beginning to catch on, as though no matter what you may have achieved you still seem likely to pull off anything, *even adulthood.* But as though time could stand still for you.

—You're beginning to worry me. It's more on the order of a default. But then, you know, one day I might become an astronaut!

—And I can almost believe it.

—No, really, it's useless sending a journalist into space. For Chrissake, we know enough about the *literal* side of it. Besides, I mean, what's so literal about outer space? They ought to send a poet. A priest. Someone with a temperament. Seems to me the job requires frenzy. And besides, what have I achieved?

—Personality wise I'd say you've achieved the equivalent of scaling Mount Everest.

—More like Mount Oblomov. *But even if so much as a fly invades my space I become all sorts of indignant!* Oh, come on. One ought to hope for grace, or at least a sense of humor. Or else it is the conscious ones who are most hard on themselves. It's just a pattern, like a wrinkle on the face etched by vicissitudes and circumstances none of which I had any hand in. And besides, you're rather fond of me, I think.

—*The sound of chains on snowplows. . . .*

—Oh Lydia, I wanted so much to do something remarkable with my life.

—But I think you will.

—Something marvelous, while at the same time foolhardy. To levitate or to self-combust, that is the question! To act or to endure. I've only recently gotten over it. I felt my birth was a gift, with no strings attached, as though the *mirage* of original sin did not apply to me. Because I bought into the myth whereby guilt is the detestation one feels for his parents. And because I had none, I thought I was free. I wanted to compose songs, but in a fashion, in a spirit, completely removed from anyone else. Just to please myself. Instead, and far from anything remarkable, I found myself snared in this vicious woof called life. I was convinced, there, for a time, that there was some arcane wisdom, some system or *truth,* some secret to my fate whereby I acquire weatherability against the storm of trial and tribulation. But no matter how expert I became, at hating, or understanding, or forgiving, even, I could not quite unsnare myself. And now I cannot shake the thought, but, that it cannot but amount to some narcissistic hallucination. The greatest surrender is to accept that we are wrong, to accept that what's become of life and civilization, *what's become of our lives,* to accept how this is wrong and yet give up our hands in mock rationalizations, and adopt the motto whereby money and family and *celebrity* are what wins us our freedom. Well perhaps for some, but who's kidding who? The only thing of which we own a profound sense, is of our *unfreedom.* You understand me, don't you, Lydia? That I cannot bring a child into this world? That I cannot accept that I should be responsible for another's having to experience this woolly lot of nonsense? Is any of it worth the bother? I know, *love* perhaps. And perhaps even that hard beauty that is the broken heart. But that too, that too is a convention, an artform, a monogamy. All we have are our frayed and exhausted and exhausting conventions.

That the woman should be endowed with this capability for multiple orgasms, and that it should serve none save the he-beasts should gang-rape her and she would know some pleasure by the various cocks! *We are wild dogs. Wild ghetto dogs on the prowl! HIDE YOUR DAUGHTERS! GOOD DECENT PEOPLE! KEEP SAFE YOUR DAUGHTERS AND WIVES!*

I went berserkers. I ran screaming up Third Avenue, my arms flailing crazily above my head. My coat flew off. My scarf flew off. Lydia flew off in the opposite direction. The sidewalk was packed with window shoppers, they obediently moved aside to let me through. I got about three blocks, just to 86th, when a police car cut me off. I thought they were a little rough on me. It was unnecessary, cracking my ribs. But on the whole it wasn't too awful. Actually, as the evening wore on, they were quite apologetic about kneeing me in the ribs that way. I had a friendly conversation with the two apprehending officers at the hospital. They were pretty entertained by my rationale for exhibiting such behavior. They said the best they could do would be to treat me as they would a homeless person. They said I could escape as soon as I felt up to it.

The second college I attended was this somewhat dilapidated though venerable institution located on the Upper East Side of Manhattan. It was here that I encountered the black lesbian feminist warrior, and it was during this time that I fell out of contact with Lydia.

I became a staff writer on the leading college paper, and because I lacked seniority I was putting in late hours doing paste-ups and galley proofs. At the paper we did everything the old-fashioned way, including, besides all the practical to-do, the work of proofreading. There were several rather toilsome steps for a copy to meet before it could be given to press. And so although the bulk of our copy came in clean on text file, when I was not cutting and pasting I was printing out and proofing someone else's article. This series of procedures was also meant to help familiarize the new staffer with the tone and style of the paper. All the hours I would otherwise have spent with Lydia were now being given to the copy desk. There were whole weeks, that so crammed first semester, during which we could see each other only once. We were meeting at a coffee shop on Madison, which was not entirely convenient for her as at this time she was teaching at Columbia. We were always being foiled by the weather, it seemed. Some impending rain or snowstorm kept our meetings hurried and abrupt. And nor were we at our apartments much, we had most of our exchanges via the answering machine. She spoke of how she was finding her niche and mentioned this Comparative Literature professor who was helping her adjust to the demands. I described for her my classes and my position at the paper and this article I was drafting on the cultural upheavals of the 1960s. We were no longer sharing intimate concerns about ourselves, instead we were describing our predicaments, and this was obvious to both of us, although for my part it was not so much intentional as rather charily going along with what her state of mind would or could tolerate of me. More and more it was difficult, and ever obvious, for me to be any sort of way other than feeling constricted and befuddled. I had the feeling she was worried I would cross the line into what was now her guarded terrain. And this was frustrating, and exasperating, because I had no choice but to go along with whatever her mood required—but just to ensure she would remain accessible to me. It is, or so it is for the temper, a bull-in-a-china-shop situation, because you feel all bulky and ungainly, and you must slalom, for Chrissake, the most delicate and precarious course. It was ever my intention, and yet I was unable to tell her so, that I would *be,* or, *in time come to behave,* in whatever manner she was needing. Just don't play the end-game card, just don't disappear on me.

I made acquaintances at the paper, just as I happened to do during classes, but for the most part I was keeping to myself. If an impression was to be made, I figured, it best be that of a competent colleague, and what's more my position on the staff wasn't stable, I was starting my probationary period. After meetings we all pretty much went our separate ways, one or two other staffers would remain with me in the office, but they, as did I, had projects to see to, so whatever socializing happened to go on was really by way of our co-operative efforts. There was an attractive and ever competent young woman, her name was Susanna, who supervised my procedures. I got the hang of things pretty quickly. We had few opportunities to speak frankly but when we did I could tell we were becoming friends. It was difficult, for everyone, to begin a conversation.

Now ours was not the only publication at the school, there were at least a dozen others. The system was to have you become a part of whatever publication served or attracted your interests. Every interest, or group, or *parochialism,* as I later came to regard them, had its own and rather extremist monthly or semimonthly organ of opinion. For instance, the gays had their own paper, as did the lesbians and as did the feminists, and as of course did the Latinos and the blacks and the Jews. The Christian Fellowship had theirs, and indeed here I learned existed a powerful intervarsity federation. Even the physically challenged had their own and rather antagonistic newsletter of opinion. It was called, *The Digitept.* The computer club had a monthly. It was called, *Compoohter.* And the conservatives, of course, they had an anti-PC, anti-*deconstruction* monthly called, *The New Cynicism.* But even the students-overweight, they had their own, and exclusive, semimonthly, entitled, *Avoirdupois.* And there were intercampus coalitions, too, like on the order of a united oppressed peoples. I suppose when the situation called for it, that was the cue to come together under the banner of general dissent. But separately, independent of the other, and not so secretly, each group considered itself to hold the first-place victim status. It is a screwy and not all sound, methinks, phenomenon, the vying for the first-place victim status. But the main paper supposedly existed to serve everyone, *regardless of the imperfection.* And perhaps—but who can surmount such logic?—perhaps this was why an instant chill permeated the air whenever anyone began a conversation. For since we existed to serve everybody, we so feared slighting anybody—but to the degree where even mere suspicion of a prejudiced opinion would occasion emergency introspection. Being a staffer at the main paper eventually led to an internship at one of the city's newspapers. This prospect, however peripheral to my true aspirations—which were, admittedly, a mystery to me—nevertheless appealed to me.

On certain occasions, when it was appropriate—that is, when it could pass undetected by the others—Susanna would attract my eye as if to say, *now we've gone a little overboard.* We both so disliked the sense of being so obviously apolitical that we were obviously political, that we began to refer to the paper as, *The Dictaphobe.* And we conspired to begin interjecting politically incorrect commentary into our articles. Her first *interjection* read that unions make it possible for morons to earn one-hundred grand a year. She gave as an example, railroad train conductors. Her compulsory retraction read that unions make it possible for workers to earn humane salaries and benefits. I did not deem her retraction a fall from grace.

—Besides, she said, both statements are true.

For our November election issue she called the voters' attention to the rather irreverent phenomenon of sedition-minded political leaders who herd their followers into massive voting blocs in order to swing a decision. *The voting booth has become a public toilet!* the article read.

—We have simply come to lack the stomachs for single-minded greatness, she told on the evening we put that issue together.

It was apparent how relieved and grateful she was to have at last been appointed an ally, *a confederate,* as she so tagged me.

—Our tastes, she continued, our *aesthetics* bespeak a high-strung impatience, a veritable aversion for any such endeavor requiring venturesome intellectual assertion. We indulge ourselves on that sweet candy that is the seemingly innocuous, ignorant to the consequent unflattering tooth decay of the brain. *Our minds have lost their bite!* The remarkable European and American tradition of individualism and Great Persons is dissolving into something frighteningly resembling Asian collectivism. The secret as to why the Asian students fare so well in science and mathematics is simply because these particular academic endeavors are most accommodating of the collectivist mentality, whereas these same academic endeavors arouse antagonism in the individualistic mentality, which tends to remodel, remake. *Do not find dismay in your competitive instincts, but rather hone them into a verbal martial art,* she told. The movement to remove competitiveness from our classrooms is inimical to me. To eradicate the competitive instincts from our students by neutralizing the curricula seems downright seditious and ought to be combated as such. Do not acquiesce in a pleasing, drowse-inducing conformity, but rather let your exceptional individualism be the bulwark against the collectivism that would like Mephistopheles promise the undeliverable in exchange for your soul. We are history's accumulated sloth, she continued. We are pampered, Stephen, *don't you get it?* We have chucked learned intellect and learned sensibility for quick viscera and short-lived pop. Our popular tastes and attainments do not but confess the most spent and deficient expression of human intellect and sensibility ever. *Oh! For the great good fortune of having had a seat before one William James or Bertrand Russell.* Ours is not an age of great educators, Stephen. And so we must adapt ourselves. Ours is not the Golden Age. *Ours is not the American Century!* Just so much of our heritage has gone rancid from neglect. The very meat and drink of it! One must be uttermost mindful of her manners with regard to anyone she may happen to meet, she told, as everyone nowadays comes preequipped with their very own personal time-honed sack of emotional contact explosives, and indeed whatever may be said, albeit in however magnanimous a temper, may just as well be construed so as to detonate a hate-bomb. We are just so aware of the differences which separate us. We have straitened ourselves beyond all reasonable semblance of affiliation. And herein lies new and multiform parochialisms!

Soon enough, she was reprimanded for her article. As a rehabilitation she was forbidden to publish for the remainder of the semester. She was also forbidden to supervise my procedures, that is unless another staffer was present. I was let off the hook, or so they said—*they* being the faculty adviser, the editor-in-chief, and the assistant editor—because I was a freshman and was therefore impressionable. Well in the first place, I was not a freshman, I had transferred with forty-eight credits. And I was not impressionable, I told them, and I resented their patronizing me so. In that case, they said, I was on *double* probation—one more strike and they'd inform the dean, which might therefore mean my removal from the staff. The student government issued a pamphlet in which they mentioned Susanna by name and physical description. This description contained the term *WASP.* It contained her class schedule, too. And it urged all concerned students to write to the paper, and to the various deans, demanding her removal from the staff, if not her outright expulsion from the college. So much for liberal tolerance.

Now I was not all that familiar or in any way personally involved with the other members of our staff. What I at first accepted as preliminary coolness now evolved into unmistakable cold shoulders. However, I was still the last to see the paper off to press, and this position was to be taken advantage of.

There was a message on my machine. Lydia sounded upset, saying Thanksgiving plans were canceled. I had for the past two years been a guest at her parents' home in Connecticut—prior to that, I had of course always been at Aunt Gloria's. I immediately phoned her, having to listen for ten rings until she answered. She said she was in the hall, she had just locked the door and was waiting for the elevator when she heard it start to ring. She was running back to the office. She said it's 'cause she thought it might be me that she decided to pick up.

—How come your machine's not on?

—I was recording a new message and it got fouled up so I left it off.

—Oh. Okay. So what's going on? *You want to be alone? Since when?*

—Since I'm carrying three classes and have midterms on my desk.

—So we won't be together? What'll you eat? It's only one day, we needn't stay for the weekend. We'll catch a late train back. You'll have Friday and the weekend to work.

—I want to do it now.

—Then I'll be alone too.

—That's ridiculous. I thought you'd go to Aunt Gloria's.

—Did you fight with your mother?

—No.

—How's your father? Did you talk to him?

—He's fine. They're both fine.

—Did you go in today?

—I go in every day. *I have three classes plus my office hours!*

—I took a midterm today. A real snap. I published that article. It's due out next Wednesday. I thought I'd let you read it on the train.

—I'll read it Monday. I'll try to reach you over the weekend. If I can't, I'll leave a message. Right now I'm running out.

—At ten-o'clock?

—Give my love to Aunt Gloria.

It was not at all unusual for Lydia to be anxious, and to be impatient, especially with me, and especially not lately. It was not as though she had given me short shrift, and especially given what must be near overwhelming responsibilities at school. Besides, I suppose I was used to her mercurial temper, and just as she was used to mine. We had always more or less graciously granted each other the space for such intermittent flights. We never went so far as to hang up on each other but once or twice we reached saturation point and called it an early night. On such occasions I learned to appreciate the convenience, indeed the virtue, of separate apartments. And then, usually, some later on or first thing next morning, one of us phoned the other—if only to assure it wasn't end-time. Invective was reserved for third parties, third parties being everyone else. Or so it goes when you have just one best friend, and everyone else is just everyone else. Sometimes it could be melodramatic, I suppose, but then again it was what we required, or else I think things would have been otherwise. I think that, whether we appreciate it or not, whether we've knowingly brought it about ourselves or not, our situations are what they are because they are what suits us. Unhappiness and malcontentedness arise out of misplaced or misconceived priorities. I was taking this seminar on ethics, the professor was this intense Filipino and routinely his wife—an Irish woman, who just happened to have a face like Agnes Moorehead as Aunt Fanny—would sit in with us. On one occasion, during the discussion period, she made this remark that pretty much shut everyone up. She said there are occasions in life when we see clearer in darkness. After class I asked her what she meant. She said we have no control over our dreams, yet upon awakening we desire to rejoin them, to see the dream through to some outcome or resolution. She said this propensity is on account of our desire—I think her word was, *habit*—to know our futures, and furthermore of our need to feel there is some otherworldly pilot at work governing our course. She said this is delusional, that fanciful hopes in Providence or fate are a means by which we surrender control over our lives, by which we subject ourselves to an imaginary monarch, for fear of failing should we take upon ourselves the burden of control. She said the darkness corresponds to our suffering, and that suffering results from misinterpretation.

—But that's a paradox, I said. *How does clarity issue from darkness?*

—The sight to which the saying refers is hindsight. From hindsight we understand who and what we have become, and how our darkness is as much a result of our own doings as it is of the doings of others. Darkness is internal as well as external. Concentrate on changing the internal. The person who will only blame others for his suffering can never really see with opened eyes. He is as much a cause of his own darkness as anybody else may be.

She said Hermann Hesse put it best when he wrote of fate as temperament. Which is to say, if you want to change or to become master of your fate, you'll have to begin by changing or becoming master of your temperament. I suppose it's like when someone talks about *emotional intelligence,* which is really just an academic term for self-control. He's really talking about an age-old wisdom.

Work on your temperament, thereat lies your fate!

—Do you believe in God? I asked her, and at this she smiled, and a little condescendingly.

She was looking at me. And somewhat condescendingly. It was beginning to annoy me.

—*God,* she said, and furrowing her brow—which she then kept furrowed so, but as though it was paining her to speak— *has nothing whatsoever to do with ethics.*

—Well, I said, it's all rather impersonal, then.

Well I suppose she had reached her saturation point, which is one of my major effects on people. She closed her mouth and locked it shut. She unfurrowed her brow, then furrowed it up again and something fierce. At the same time she elongated her face and made her lips into this straight pale line. Her whole face beneath the eyes became this flat white wall. She looked a little comical—this face makes a caricature of herself, I thought, and mostly because with her brow all furrowed up like that it gave her these, well, these lines like plow tracks from a Thomas Hart Benton painting. It was not at all attractive, and I think it was meant to frighten me off. Which it most certainly did.

I suppose normally I would have been upset about Thanksgiving, about not being with her at all the entire weekend, but I had my article on my mind and I was preoccupied with my responses to all the consequences I imagined could result from it. I called Susanna to tell her all had gone as planned. One of her roommates answered the phone.

—Oh yes. Stephen Child. *She really likes you.*

—Thank you. That's very nice. Is she at home?

—Right now she's out breaking up with her boyfriend. Why don't you call back after midnight, she should be back by then.

—Well, *gee,* why don't you ask her to call me 'cause I'll be home the rest of the evening.

—Does she have your number?

—I think she does. I gave it to her.

—My name's Kate, by the way.

—You have a lovely telephone presence, Kate.

—Thank you. I'm writing down that you called. I'm sure she'll see it.

She called a little past midnight. She was afraid I might be sleeping.

—No. I'm just resting. Staring at the ceiling. Sort of *stargazing,* you know?

—I do that too sometimes.

—Once your eyes become adjusted to the dark, you can imagine all sorts of things. I usually see these constellations.

—Are you sure I didn't wake you?

—No. Really. See, I used to have this toy, well actually it belonged to my cousin, I used to play with all his toys. Anyway, I had this toy that was this sort of flashlight-projector thing, and it projected images onto the ceiling. *Stars, constellations, galaxies.*

—I know that toy. It projected *comics,* too.

—Right. . . . So, I wanted to say, all has gone as planned.

—Outstanding, Stephen! So listen, I'll be going home on Wednesday morning. Have you made your plans for Thanksgiving yet?

—I suppose I'll be going to my aunt's.

—Oh. When're you leaving?

—Well my aunt lives just a few blocks away.

—Oh.

—So I suppose I'll walk over around noon-time. I'll watch the football games with my cousins. You know, the usual.

—Are you with them every year? I mean, do you have Thanksgiving dinner with your family? I'm going home to Massachusetts until Sunday. I'd like to see you before then.

—Are you coming in tomorrow?

—I have a ten-thirty class, but I'm just dropping off my midterm assignment. Then I have some shopping to do. *And of course I will not be stopping by the paper.* Would you like to come home with me for the holiday?

—*Susanna.*

—My parents have a farm in the Berkshires. Did you want to say something? I thought you said my name.

—You have a lyrical name. *Susanna.*

—I like *your* name. Saint Stephen was the first martyr.

—You know, Susanna, how we have descriptive names for each of the distinctive historical periods. For example, *Dark Ages, Renaissance.*

—Of course.

—Well I think we should designate a *Lyrical* period.

—Oh. You mean in the past? You don't mean the 1960s.

—I think nineteenth-century America, or maybe, the turn-of-the-century, was a *lyrical* period. Because of the hopefulness, as *hope* is a sort of spontaneous feeling, a *lyrical* feeling.

—I'd like to have you home with me.

—That sounds very nice.

I suppose I should give you some idea of the appeal my Susanna held for me, how the attraction, while it was certainly sensual, was in no wise entirely sexual but promised a further dimension of comfort and security. This further dimension, experience had taught me, was essential if I was to experience the feelings of vulnerability and susceptibility that are the prerequisites of enchantment. Susanna had a big head, with long, wavy auburn hair, like a big orange mackerel-striped barn cat of the All-American variety. And she had freckles on her nose. And she always wore old Levi's, slung low on her hips, and scuffed blucher mocs and oxford shirts. And even when she wore her bulky crewneck you could tell she had no bra on underneath. Invariably my impulse was to wrestle her down in a joyously uninhibited hug. Even her appetite was healthy—another aspect of her overall hope-inspiring presence. At Thanksgiving dinner, and much to the delight of her parents, she consumed a good mountain of food. Her father, Mr. Frazer, or *Bill* as he so preferred, graciously kept the conversation going so that no one felt uncomfortable.

—Stephen? Will you let us in on this article Susanna's been teasing us about?

—I'd be happy to, *Bill.* My article concerns the 1960s, and all the cultural upheaval that transpired as a result of the cleft that was splitting our society. Basically this cleft was a burgeoning selfishness, *but that's not the point of the article.* The article doesn't focus on the street or on civil rights or on debates in Congress but rather aims to explain the tumult that shook the middle-class American family.

And then it occurred to me that the Frazers must have come of age around the 1960s. I thought they might be applying some special insight to what I was about to report. It is a curious phenomenon, exists unto us Americans, and especially where concerns the 1960s. People who have come of age during that time are as though initiated into an exclusive club, and are thereby equipped or certified to hold the last word on everything from LSD to the 1968 Democratic National Convention. Indeed were you to bring together every man, woman and child who was present at the 1969 Woodstock music festival, why here you would have today's equivalent of the Freemasonry. *Who do you think invented networking?*

—The article, I continued, maintains the opinion that they, *they* being the sons and daughters of the middle class, had it too good, *too many good possibilities!* And consequently, you see, this was bad for the species. You see, in order to evolve, the species requires struggle, *and struggle ought to always result in growth.* The species has intrinsically the necessity to evolve, but this evolving requires struggle, and where struggle is not prevalent, the species will indeed seek it out, *nay invent it!* The species will set its own height, however artificial or contrived, and then attempt to surmount it. But the species is laden with psychology, and on that account it is subject to, or susceptible to, deception. Now, having had it so good, and sensing in their loins, if not in their brains, the lack of and therefore need for struggle, the species looks to its provider as the source and cause of its stymie. The provider is the culprit, you see, because the provider has provided too much. *Too many good possibilities!* So toward the provider, then, does it, the offspring of the species, funnel all its frustration. All those hard-working parents, going off to the office in their suits and ties and stockings, *going off to the big bad corporation.* But now something interesting happens. By some quirky leap of logic, but really, such logic, it will forever escape me, by some quirky leap of logic anything corporate, executive, judicial, legislative *nay* institutional, is made out to be the big daddy of all provision, and toward all these is funneled their frustration. The object of conflict, the battle-ground of struggle, is in a quirky little way transferred from the hearth, from the domestic altar, from the bosom of the family, onto the pillars of society. And so, it is not only the parents toward whom all their frustration is funneled, but it is toward the suit and the tie and the stockings, and all these things were made over to represent. *The Establishment!*

There was silence. Then Bill's eyes turned to Mrs. Frazer, Mrs. Frazer turned to Susanna, and Susanna came up with this terrific Cheshire-Catesque grin.

—*Simply mad!* she remarked clasping her hands at her chin, her elbows on the table and her legs reaching out 'til her toes were mingling with mine.

Afterwards, after helping clear the table, she took me outside. We followed a path into the woods. It was pitch black in all directions. The stars were out, but they were blocked by the tallest pines. She held the flashlight to show on the boughs. I was fascinated and I suppose she sensed I was trembling a little. She let her arm around my waist and I had mine around her shoulders. I was content to just be held that way. We were investigating the shadows on the boughs. Then she lowered the flashlight and we kissed and hugged. And after that and for the rest of the weekend we kissed and cuddled at every opportunity.

I'll never let go of the Frazer farm. Especially their stables and barn. I saw the swallows, darting from the eaves. And beyond the barn I saw forest, dense, serried pine forest. Or else the wood was so far off, it appeared a surge of dark lake water. I told Susanna what I thought of this and she swore we shared the same impression.

Sunday evening I played Lydia's message. She said she'd called Aunt Gloria's Thanksgiving day and then asked who was the friend I was visiting. I was glad she wanted to know. She said she'd meet me only it was at this place where she was meeting someone else. Of course I knew who it was she was meeting, it was this Comparative Literature professor.

Probably it was the turkey, or probably it was Lydia, or probably it was having to face all the fallout from my article. Anyhow, I woke up with a headache. I took two aspirins with some toast. And I was crying in the shower. It wasn't so much the headache as it was my feeling sorry for myself. My staffmates at the paper were unable to pretend to the humor in politics and human nature. I felt my taste for the entire situation drain out of me, and the aftertaste was bitter. To disobey the party line was to become anathema. Susanna's words were resounding in my head. I began constructing a defense—not on account of how I snuck it in, as I was due to publish something anyway, and besides, the editor-in-chief had okayed my topic, but more on account of how I gave a certain slant to what I took to be free range.

I skipped stopping off at the paper and instead went straight for class. I passed some paper stands and saw they all were empty, but as though my article had caused a run on the paper. And as though I had set myself up for a reprimand. Then as I made my way a voice from down the hall called after me. It was my editor-in-chief, she said a Professor Lorry wished to see me in her office, *the office of Black Studies.* I asked what about. *It's about your article!* And it struck me who this Professor Lorry was. She had described herself in an interview as a black lesbian feminist warrior. And she had the reputation of being fearless.

I began to perspire. I thought of calling Susanna. And then I thought of calling Lydia. And then I thought of going shopping. I thought of meeting Aunt Gloria and going to the stores and to lunch and a movie. I felt my whiskers and I thought I should have shaved. *Why didn't I shave?* I thought, *why wasn't I with Lydia Thanksgiving?* And I knew she was seeing this professor. *Why does she want me to meet him?*

I was waiting outside Lorry's office. There seemed to be a party going on inside, and I felt as though they knew who I was, *and then the thought of them having a laugh on me.* I began to tremble. When she arrived I was surprised by her appearance. She was younger than I had expected. She was small, and dressed somewhat conservatively, I thought. Her skirt was to just above her knees, I know 'cause when she arrived I was sitting on the floor and the first thing I noticed was her legs. It was as though she helped me to my feet, 'cause she reached to shake my hand and I held her as I rose. And then her face was right in my face, and I saw this woman was beautiful. *This woman has a beautiful face.* And I thought, how so much beauty, even if antagonistic, how so much beauty cannot but assuage. Then in the sweetest, Southern accent, she addressed me.

—Stephen Child?

—Yes. Professor Lorry?

And did she sense how I was trembling?

—Come on inside. May I call you Stephen? You may call me Tammy.

About a dozen young women—both black and white, and all for the most part normal-looking—cleared out of her office. Like a fool I tried to make eye contact with them, but they all just hurried by.

—I read your article, she said.

I looked to see if it was on her desk.

—I have it right here.

She had it clipped out of the paper.

—I read it a couple of times, in fact. It's almost something I'd expect to find in *The New Cynicism.*

—I'm not on their staff.

—And no one on that staff can write as well as you do.

—Thank you. Do you read *The New Cynicism?*

—You mean for comic relief?

She was looking over the article. I suppose she was trying to decide where to begin. I thought maybe she'd just wished to size me up a little, to see how hostile I was. I thought maybe she'd just wished to show how beautiful she was. I thought maybe I'd go supine on her desk as though it were some ancient altar crying *HEAL ME! HEAL ME, O!* And I felt like I wanted to cry, but as though I were before my confessor, and about to receive absolution.

—Would I be too far off base were I to consider your methodology, oh, *speculative?*

And despite her question, I think she was trying to be peaceable.

—Do you disapprove of my method?

—It is a legitimate method, say, on those occasions where there are no facts to be had. However, where it concerns the 1960s, and the entire civil rights era, for that matter, there are more facts available to the scholar than any one scholar can possibly make use of. You chose to ignore every one of them.

—Did I at least give you something to think about?

—You put yourself into the shoes of the women and men who marched and were put upon by fire hoses and police dogs, *and then you give me something to think about!*

—I do not mean to invalidate that experience.

—Look. I don't want to make you late for your class. You have obvious talent, Stephen. You owe it to yourself to carefully consider what you choose to put into print. Write another article. I'll help you with the references. *Put your talent to some beneficial use.*

Saying good-bye to her, and again shaking her hand, I felt I'd won the privilege of kissing her cheek. I felt the need to make some show of affection. I didn't, however, and only because I was uncertain. But I'm not entirely certain she would not have appreciated it. She had missed the point of my article. Perhaps she could not, or would not, acknowledge the legitimacy of my complaint. And it was not my place, nor did I have the strength, to enlighten her. My struggle was not her struggle. Her struggle was entirely political. I needed only to overcome myself.

I was late getting over to meet Lydia. I worried a little over whether she would wait for me. I found a copy of the paper and I headed out for Second Avenue. I was really perspiring. And it was cold outside. And I'd forgotten my gloves outside Lorry's office. I turned off Second for 87th, and I found her, and *him,* waiting on the stoop of an old brick townhouse. The townhouse had scaffolding outside it, and the workers were chipping away at the old cement. As I approached he met me with this rather inquisitive—and somewhat invasive, I thought—expression, stroking this rather Freudesque facial hair of his, but as though he were about to begin psychoanalysis on me. Lydia knows I can't stand guys like this. I can't stand any sort of highbrow scrutiny, and if only because I'm so uncertain of myself, because I've never been content with who I was or where I was at, and so I dread the thought of someone, some amateur, psychoanalyzing me down to some neat category or proposition. It's not that I wasn't in on living for the moment, and appreciating who I was and what I had to offer, I understood these things pretty well, I thought. But rather it was this *prospective* thing, that one day—and in this life, with any luck—that one day I'd get a handle on myself, I'd get a handle on myself so far as what really mattered was concerned, and from there I'd be better able to make judgments, and to act like a decent human being, for Chrissake.

I preferred to observe him indirectly, trying not too rudely to avoid this penetrating facial hair of his, but it was difficult, and what was making it even more difficult was that he was bald on top, and his head was shining. I didn't want him to think I was noticing his baldness, and if only because he might hate me for it, and in retaliation steer Lydia away from me. I tried to imagine Freud, looking to see if *he* was bald. And I thought, *this guy has to be Jewish. Christ, a Jewish intellectual. And a professor, to boot! Just what I needed.* And he was tall, taller than both of us. He was a lot older, too. Now Lydia had eight years over me, and that in itself had always nettled me. This guy looked to be pushing sixty. *Wow. Lydia.* He was respectable-looking, nevertheless, I suppose, with the tassels on his glossy loafers, and his cuffs being inch-and-a-half, and with his camel Burberrys duffle coat, and then this nicely broken-in leather brief case. I stood there, with my ragged backpack full of books and that ridiculous paper flapping in my hand, and the ink transferring onto my fingers, alternating in feeling between real silly school boy and how ever to compete with this man.

—Stephen? he said.

Meanwhile Lydia was just standing there, mum. I couldn't bring myself to look at her.

—Yes sir, I replied.

And Chrissake, *I said sir!* I couldn't believe myself, how unprepared I was for this. I put out my ice-cold hand. He hesitated somewhat, and then he murmured something, and then he thrust out his hand, and with his glove on, no less, and shook all hell out of my wrist. I gave the paper to Lydia. I still couldn't look at her face.

—Well I'm on my way, I said. Just passin' through.

Lydia said nothing. She didn't even say hello, let alone give me a kiss hello. And I felt all sorts of embarrassment. And then I did something really potentially brainless. After a few stoops or so I turned around to see if they were watching me. I saw them entering the townhouse.

It was a long walk home, down to 56th at York. At first I couldn't think about it, the whole scenario resisted whatever angle I tried to penetrate it from. I was watching myself in all the windows and fingering the fluff inside my pockets. I was smiling, too. And oddly, I suppose, I was feeling a rush of euphoria. I felt aloof, even. I felt as though I had just fallen in love and I was thinking, *isn't this inappropriate?* I was enjoying the walk and my reflection in all the storefront windows. And I was thinking I might go shopping, into Bloomingdale's, and maybe check out their duffle coats. And then I felt a little anxious, and for a moment I thought it was morning and I panicked on how I might be late for class. And then I did something real unusual, I checked the street sign to see where I was at. I usually have this sixth sense about my location, in fact whenever I'm asked to give directions I usually do so by the compass point, saying how far to proceed in north or south or east or west and, really, this drives the tourists crazy.

The first thing I thought, feeling this way, was to somehow get back to Lydia, but I just as instantly knew how ridiculous that was. I tried, I tried by imitating him, I tried to decipher that murmur he'd made, but all I could come up with was *wanderer, wandering, wondering.* I thought of them going to make love, and this made me panicky again. Each time I thought of Lydia's behind I had to stop to catch my breath and regain my balance. I rested awhile at a parking meter. At one point I rested on a stoop and took out a book and tried to read for my homework. Everything, however, and much to my dismay, was ripe for the association. I had accustomed myself to seeing her behind in every melon on the street. There were grocers everywhere. And I think I lost control of my facial muscles. I thought I was smiling, but when I looked at my reflection up close I in fact realized a terrible grimace. I also noticed there was gook in my eyes, and I wondered if I'd been crying.

When you're a boy you hear all sorts of myths about the girls, like how the girls can't just make love, that they require an emotional attachment. I had since learned that this was indeed true for the girls but that for women it's another case entirely. I also knew that where Lydia was concerned making love was a real team sport.

When I got home I hid myself under the covers. I was instinctively curled up into a foetus. I tried to will myself to disappear, and when that didn't work I said a prayer. *Nothing flashy, please. No white smoke and applause. Just a soft and quiet disappearance.* I was sobbing pretty deeply. I thought about the phone and thought, *what miracle, what miracle if only she would call.* I swore aloud, of how I would not be possessive. I swore to Christ I'd have it any way she needed. If only she would call to check up on me.

I think it's so for everyone, at least when you're a kid, that you have this pretty reasonable sense of immortality and immunity, a sort of psychological shield against the belief that anything catastrophically bad can happen to you or to your family. Things like cancer, and divorce, and alcoholism, or like losing a brother or a sister or a friend when they're so young and supposed to last forever, or like watching your father lie helpless on the ground and then the ambulance taking him away. These things defeat that shield, and growing up is just so much realization that you're not immune, you're not immortal, anything can happen to anyone and at any time and . . . *that's that.*

Everything is as it ought to be. Make no mistake. *Pale veal cutlet. Famished little calf, fettered to a stall.* Everything. The priests. The police. Psychiatrists.

Chained to an oppressive whim, as poplars to nature's wind.

My antics. I have these recollections. I am unable to undo them. I cringe, each time they happen. I am afterthoughts too late to be useful. I am Jacob, wrestling with an afterthought. Sometimes I shake my head, but violently so. I will rattle my brain. I try to rattle myself out of consciousness. The things I've done, the situations I've been into, whole sets of circumstances that I've undergone, that I seem to have dreamt myself into. I cringe for yesterday. *I cringe for today.* I smile, and I cringe, *for oh! how conspicuous.* And yea, this oblivion, 'tis not mine alone. I am Usher, forever pale. I am Usher, easily bleeding. *And as soon as I am touched, I respond.* I am Ruthven, with a vein, with a vane, with a hair, but as though I bear a smudge on my forehead. *It gives me away every time.*

And this is the asylum of mirrors?

I know you like that. Will you credit me?

What do you suggest?

A new head. Change the slide!

You change it.

I am a child, and I am alone inside this magnificent church. I know this church, this is where we held the Mass for my friend Tommy. I am kneeling in a pew off to the right side of the altar. A huge white column is situated between myself and the altar, obstructing my line of vision. A priest approaches the altar but he has disappeared behind the column, and although I can hear him speaking, I cannot hear the words to his prayer. I do not think he knows that I am there and I have the sense that I am spying on him. I am moving my jaw up and down, and as I do, my teeth are falling from my mouth, one by one, into my hand which I hold beneath my chin to catch them. When my teeth are all out, I begin speaking: The light! As though it has passed through the tears of Christ, the tears which upon touching the earth are prismatic crystals. The light! As though it has passed through the blood of Christ, the blood which upon touching the earth is hyacinthine gems. The light! As though it has passed through the eyes of Christ, the eyes which upon touching the earth are gold dodecahedrons. The light! As though it has passed through the body of Christ, the body which upon touching the earth is pearl.

"Stephen's Idyll"

The boy, let out to the garden, stood in a puddle left by the rainfall. He looked down to his feet and there he found his reflection gazing up at him. And then he saw the sun's reflection shimmering there beside his own. He raised his eyes and with his palm above his brow he studied the yellow disk as it was amid the great blue space. His skin was warmed. He closed his eyes and placed his palm atop his head feeling the warmth absorbed by his hair. Now a breeze traveled by thick with the various herbs of the garden. Never before had he the pleasure of enjoying the aromas so freely. Sensing them so made him sigh and he opened his eyes. For a moment he thought he would see the aromas and imagined them a likeness to the rainbow. The ground was puddly. From puddle to puddle he went, standing in each and seeing in each reflection the sun shimmering beside his image.

So many coves, or lagoons. Whichever is characteristic of lakes.

Must we be exact?

Yes. I want to be exact.

In that case, lagoon. Its root is lacus, *for lake.*

I am a child. And I am playing upon the banks of a lagoon. The water at this lagoon is crowded with giant lily pads. The pads are of greenish heart-shaped leaves and upon them, at their centers, sits a burst of yellow petals forming a tea cup. Now this corolla of these flowers corresponds to the corona of the sun. And as the frogs sip their tea out of these cups, the planets sip theirs by the edge of the sun.

That's very nice.

Thank you. I know I tend to overdo things. It takes me one whole minute to turn off the stove. I know you think I'm complusive, but it may be just a fear of catching fire.

You're the one putting that idea into my head. Let me think for myself.

On certain days, weather permitting, and at a certain hour of the day, a sunbeam but such as though it were the extending of a divine transport, fills this lagoon as though it were especially intended for these lily pads at this particular lagoon. Now my father owned a yellow canoe. And as I played upon the banks of this lagoon, just out of step of the moist ground, I heard the lily pads swishing to the sides. I turned to see my father paddling towards me, and through this brilliant sunbeam. That was how it must have happened. Yet I remember it differently. I turned to behold my father glissading to Earth upon a resplendent sunbeam.

What is the significance of the boy in the garden?

The rainfall is the storm of trial and tribulation. The puddle is the remembering of such storm, and the reflection in the puddle is hindsight or what we may see of ourselves in the past. The many puddles are our many experiences. The many reflections are how we may learn of ourselves as we look back upon such experiences.

And the herbs, the aromas, the rainbow?

The herbs are the virtues. The aromas are the clues or guide or correct interpretations to these virtues. The rainbow is hope of salvation.

And who is the boy?

And who is the boy. If the process is to be successful, you must approach it with the openness of a child. This openness allows for a calmness of mind, a sort of freedom. It is the being free of prejudice, a casting off of narrow-mindedness. A casting off of the collective guilt.

Did you love Susanna?

Oh yes! I told her my life story. She graduated that year and was accepted into the FBI academy. She nearly pleaded with me to apply with her. She came up to visit often and on each occasion we did nothing but make love and eat turkey sandwiches. Susanna was an extraordinarily healthy girl. I can still sense her so vividly. Her eyes were an Impressionist's green, and her skin the softness of rain water. I'll never really let go of her. Of course she made it possible for me to survive all that fallout after Lydia. I was having the shakes damn regularly. There really is a sort of sexual healing that goes on. Susanna was sincerity. And now that I've remembered her for you, I miss her.

"My Jewish Wolf of the Steppes"

Barry was religious. He wore his yarmulke full-time. He served for two years in the Israeli army, that's how he acquired his broken nose. He said they do that to toughen you up. . . .

—It's not necessarily a hostile act. It's more a rite of passage.

He contributed some articles to the paper, and he supplied his own photographs, all of which he had taken and developed himself. He did a series on communal life at a kibbutz from the perspective of an outsider, finally offering his criticisms by way of relating his own disinclinations to join. It was a frank and self-revealing appraisal, I thought. He told me he was torn between the longing to belong and an aversion to the idea of conformity. He said this applied to everything, including the prospect of his joining our staff.

Barry was a transient student, he would take time off between semesters, sometimes to travel, sometimes to work, and sometimes to study. His major was philosophy, and he had all these different methods of critique at his disposal. His favorite philosopher was Friedrich Nietzsche, a German who he said was far ahead of his time in foreseeing the dissolution of Western values and spirituality. He said that Nietzsche could not accept a supernatural or revelationist basis for morality and so constructed this idea of *eternal recurrence* whereby we better watch out what we do as we are bound to repeat it again and again endlessly. Nietzsche, he said, could not fathom himself out of this idea of being trapped in an eternally recurring cycle and at last had a nervous breakdown. He said if only Nietzsche had been a believing Christian he could then have accepted that Christ was a unique historical event and that therefore *He* was the only way out. He said that Nietzsche's rejection of Christian philosophy was probably entirely political, or at the least a matter of taste, and that Nietzsche believed the answers could be found back among the Greeks, back before Christian philosophy was formed.

I was not so much impressed by Nietzsche as I was with Barry's forthrightness. He usually showed up around three- or four-o'clock which just happened to coincide with my schedule. He liked to offer advice on how to arrange a neat page. Everything he said fit perfectly. And then we'd help ourselves to coffee and talk until the office got too crowded.

—Nietzsche tore the veil off of our basic drives, he broke through the surface of consciousness, he told me. Nietzsche theorized how behind everything we do lies the more often than not unconscious motive for power and influence. According to Nietzsche, our underlying drive is not for self-preservation, but for influence in our field of being, our field of endeavor. Given the type of organism we are, we must expend energy, but we do so primarily to gain dominance, to gain power and influence over our environment, *which includes other people.* Self-preservation is incidental to this.

I was somewhat acquainted with the names and some of the trends and ideas associated with the philosophers he mentioned. While at music school I had lessons on the form of German lieder, and I became familiar with the lyrics of Heinrich Heine, and Johann Wolfgang von Goethe who wrote The Erl-King which Franz Schubert then wrote this terrific piano music for and made into a famous song. It was while reading up on these songs and their cultural milieu that I came across the names of some eighteenth- and nineteenth-century philosophers.

I was impressed with Barry's fluency. And most importantly his seriousness. When he spoke there was genuine passion in his voice, as though everything depended on his getting it right. I often wondered if people thought this about *me.* I know I wanted them to.

—I understand this drive, I said, especially concerning situations where, say, a political power vacuum has occurred. Under such circumstances the majority, and fair and able people, will do nothing waiting for someone to come forward and take control of the situation, and that person who does come forward is more often than not a domineering, boldly assertive and charismatic sort who, again, more often than not, seizes control in the manner of a despot. You know, I have observed a curious tendency in myself, a predisposition. I see it in recollections of my childhood, and indeed I have known it all my life. As a child I felt a violent aversion to joining the crowd, but I did not wish to amass followers or to attract attention to myself. I just enjoyed being alone. I preferred the position of the outsider. It was what made me comfortable, what came naturally to me, what suited me best. My friends and teachers decided that I was either afflicted or stuck-up, but that was not the case at all. I know that from my early childhood I was able to have these *conversations* going on inside my head, I was able to imagine or to project one or several interlocutors at a time, and I was able to carry on these *conversations* with them. But understand, Barry, these were not only *conversations,* these were debates and arguments I was having, I was reasoning on issues and controversies, and I was coming up with positions and perspectives on things, and mostly on people, on the psychology of people, like, as to what they were about and what I could expect from them, but so as to have a sense of what was reliable and predictable about them. But most importantly, and this takes the cake, I was defending myself, I was justifying myself and my reactions, I was defending my feelings and my opinions, but as though I had this father confessor in my head, *let's call it conscience,* and he was forever taking me to task, and not only for whatever I may have said or thought or done, but merely because I was who I was, and because I had this ability to see into people and to figure them out and to know what was reliable and predictable about them, as though this in itself, as though by virtue of this ability alone, I was *ipso facto* separate, separate and different from the other people, and I would suffer be-cause of this. And so from this I always managed to form my own interpretations of things, to say the least. And I would argue with people. With the grownups! To try to persuade them to accept my point of view. *Can you imagine how hard I made it for myself?* And growing up, my heroes were all these intense loners, but not the serial-killer types, I mean the lonely geniuses, the visionaries driven insane by the futility of it all. *I was always rooting for the mad scientist!* I always identified with the outcast, and not by virtue of his being especially maladjusted but more by virtue of his having been rejected. *Can you imagine how hard I made it for myself?*

—Yes I can, Stephen. I know and I understand.

—I'm not claiming this makes me a saint. I'm not claiming this means I'm unique. Only, I was not so fortunate as to have grown up in an environment where this was appreciated of me. Rather, I was considered something of a pain in the neck. I was not fortunate enough to have known any grownups who had anything like an imagination, or the sophistication, or the intuition, or indeed the energy, to have seen, to have appreciated, that I required special attention.

—It sounds so much like my own experience. I know from my own life everything you're saying. And certainly it accounts for my own aversion to the idea of conformity. It's not that I cannot see the beauty or the validity in other perspectives. On the contrary! I just preferred, and like you say, it was *natural* for me, I just preferred to enjoy the proceedings from a distance. *I was not trying to be aloof!* Quite the contrary. *I was undergoing an inner struggle to make of myself a happy conformer!* My friends, and my father especially, labeled me a skeptic. *And I don't necessarily refute that label.*

—When I say that I enjoyed being alone, you must understand how my *enjoyment* was such that, it was as though I was giving in to an addiction. But I've since come to trust that it was nothing of the sort but a sort of *instinct* that was guiding me, informing my attitude.

—And this is why it is important to understand, or as I like to say, *to master,* our childhood experiences. *What we are now depends so much on what, and how, we were back then.* This is the first principle to realize! I'm relieved to know you have considered these things! You are a man after my own heart, Stephen.

—Thank you, Barry. That's a lovely compliment. Yes, I have considered them, I have considered them repeatedly and in ever finer detail. But of course, then, there is always the danger of *retching* whenever one regurgitates his youth!

—I know. *We can choke on our own spew!*

—I think, yes, that's what I am, a skeptic. I'm a skeptic too. I am skeptical of everything that challenges my personal liberty and self-determination!

—Well there it is. . . . What's your major?

—I haven't exactly declared one yet. I'm sort of pretending it's gonna be journalism.

—Do you want to teach? *Or do you want to write for a newspaper?*

—I don't think I want to teach. And I'm not so convinced about journalism. It seems like just another ideology. There's this *news-world logic* out there that sort of runs counter to my conscience.

—I know what you mean.

—And the whole idea of writing in *columns.* . . . I don't know what I want to do. I don't know why I'm taking journalism, except that it's something I have an interest in, and until I can make a decision, or a commitment. It's by no means my first love, I can tell you that.

—I think you would appreciate reading Nietzsche. Have you considered taking some philosophy courses?

—I have an ethics seminar with Professor Torrez, if that counts for anything.

—I know Torrez.

—Do you know his wife?

—Are you kidding?

—I must say, she does strike me as something of an atheist.

—I've read her articles. Her position is perfectly clear. She believes that humankind has reached a stage where religion has become detrimental to progress. She thinks the *concept* of God is obsolete. Personally, I'm not so sure God is just an *concept.* Are you religious? *If you don't mind me asking.*

—I don't mind. *Gee.* . . . There's not much religion, or rather, *church going,* in my family, or, that is, in my upbringing. It's there but it's sort of unconscious. My mother's side is Catholic and my father's is Episcopalian. I don't think the two sides ever really made an issue of it, but then probably as a result of that, no one ever claimed me for their own church, *but that probably says more about me than it does about our religiousness.* When I did go to church, like on Christmas Eve, I went to a Catholic church, and this is only because my friends were Catholic, and I was going to church with my friends. I don't go to church at all any more. But I do believe in God. Without God everything is meaningless. Without God everything is terrible. Actually, even with God things are terrible, but at least with God there's hope. That seems like a default position, doesn't it? Probably of all the forms of belief in God, of all the rational propositions it takes, that is the least valid one. Or else it's the belief of a skeptic.

My friend was silent now. He made no reply. In his stillness I could see him growing introspective, right before my eyes. I think we both could have just sat there, staring into space, our introspection, alas, giving way to melancholy.

—Why're you studying here? I asked him. You really want a degree from this place?

—I'm here because it's convenient. It's near my home. I don't intend to get my degree here. I wanted to matriculate. I had to be enrolled somewhere while I decided what to do. I thought I'd eventually enter NYU, and get my degree from there. I just haven't been up to making the commitment. I don't want to make the transfer and then do there what I'm doing here. Being here it's like I'm in limbo. This is my third semester here, *in two-and-a-half years.* But one thing I know for certain, if you're going to study philosophy, don't do it here, because what they do here, and what they do at other schools, too, and this is something you have to look out for, is they cover all the Greeks up to Aristotle, and then they skip over all the mediaeval grammarians and the Renaissance philosophers right up until Descartes, so you're left in the dark where it concerns Augustine and Peter Abelard and Moses Maimonides, and especially Aquinas and Scotus and the whole problem of *universals.* It's another example of how they turn ignorance into a virtue, or else the department takes it for granted that this is the stuff of specialization, but either way you lose out on a huge chunk of philosophy. If you're going to be serious about philosophy, I would suggest you transfer to a Jesuit-run college. I think there you're certainly likely to gain a background in the grammarians and in the problem of universals. Without this background, you won't have a clue as to what's really going on today, I mean especially with *deconstruction.* You know, most professors are just careerists who spend the bulk of their time performing functions *outside* the classroom in order to increase their salaries and bolster their reputations in the department. It's a rare event to encounter a professor who's a great human being, *or at least a legitimate scholar.*

And at that we were smiling again. And this was not out of any contempt, it was strictly on account of our disappointment.

—*Ours is not an age of great educators,* I said, recalling my Susanna.

Barry was roused. . . .

—Whoa! *That ought to be our rallying cry!*

—Have you by any chance seen my article?

—That is why I thought you'd be an interesting person to know! You know, everybody around here seems a bit gun-shy, *if you know what I mean.*

—So I've noticed.

—It's not good.

—No. In fact it's downright *chilling. All this dictaphobia.*

Two weeks passed by before Barry came to visit me again, in the meantime I had made the decision to transfer and I had phoned some Catholic colleges and ordered application packets from their admissions departments. I had no good reason to remain where I was, especially with Susanna gone, and especially as how I wasn't seeing or hearing from Lydia any more. And I was still having to deal with my anxiety. And the condition was becoming worse. I was now subject to unpredictable and uncontrollable fits of panic attacks.

It's more unpleasant than it sounds. Just when you believe the worst is passed, and you think you're on the road to repair, you find yourself all twisted into knots. And there's no easy antidote. No neat Alexandrian shortcut. When they say time heals all wounds, this is the wound they're talking about, but it's a long, long time, and sometimes it's a lifetime. The best approach, I think—and yes it's easier said than done, that is it's easier to have an intellectual understanding of these things than it is to persuade the emotions to go along with them—the best approach is the path of least resistance, where you let go of your anger, you release your rage and spite and you cease shaking your fists at the gods and accept the throes of despair, of uncertainty and of dread, as but another aspect, *par for the course,* of the warp and woof of life. The broken heart, the separation from the one you long for and feel you cannot live without, or even the possibility of such, must not deny you the pursuit of the commitment of love. I was amazed at how attached I had become to her. And I had taken her companionship for granted. It was a trial, keeping my mental balance, and resisting the impulse to blame and to disparage and, at my lowest, even despising her. But I could not *hate* my Lydia. It was at once the cause and relief of my crisis that I held her in such high esteem. It wasn't her fault, that I should undergo these complications in adjusting to our separation. I was predisposed to such repercussions long before she entered my life.

And why should I resent her for pursuing her affinities? I had always been free to pursue and to experience my own. And indeed, we had pursued and gained each other in the same spirit of affinity. And we agreed as to a monumental pact to allow each other the free and unhindered pursuit of our respective affinities! We in essence agreed to trust in our devotion to each other, to trust in our agreement that affinities are among the few real gifts in life.

Now you must understand that affinities are in no wise exclusively physical or sexual attractions—in no wise are they restricted to the eye. You can believe that they are chemical—chemical, or, *spiritual,* this is not the point. Affinities are an enchantment. And they cannot be manufactured or manipulated. They can only be experienced. The fundamental law of affinities is that they are transitive, and loaded with emotion and passion, and while they can lead to lifelong companionship they are by their nature ephemeral. *Affinities are dangerous!* Abelard and Heloïse shared an affinity. Affinities are in fact nature's way of bringing two persons together so that they may perform copulation and procreate—even though, how many of us are born of true affinities? Nevertheless, it is this, and the fact that we must eat, are the two principles of life on planet Earth—and then, I suppose, there's all that Nietzsche stuff, although actually I would add a third principle, the principle of acquisitiveness, the propensity to acquire, and if you want proof of this, of this fixed and ingrained characteristic of human nature, just observe your neighborhood bag lady, observe how she, although homeless, has accumulated unto her carriage a veritable closet full of objects, of useless, *and broken,* junk, but observe, how although she is in dire straits, she has not lost the will to acquire.

Now man, because he is creative, and then so easily dulled by tedium, has through the ages made of the affinity the convention of love. Love is in fact only this, but clothed in all the accouterments of custom, but clothed in the ways of convention and of etiquette. *What an exquisite artform is love!* Whether courtly or romantic love, the debutante's coming-out, and our mythologies and legends of love, and monogamy and wedlock. These are all our efforts in elevating copulation into love. The premiere note of civilization, regardless of whether you are studying Western man or the Watschandis, is, *what have they done with their sex?* It is only because the vast majority of humans are vulgarians that things have gone and will continue to go awry.

Now lest you think I'm advocating *free love,* or something along those coarse lines, I will include here a modicum of sooth gathered from the pages of the Renaissance thinker, Giordano Bruno. If the affinity is to remain, the parties of the affinity must remain continent—or else be forewarned that sexual fusion may result in a bursting of the bubble, and both parties are liable to fall prey to their temperamental predispositions, which is exactly what I was struggling with. The key to surviving this fusion is familiarity, it's friendship, it's the willingness to commit to trust. It also helps if you genuinely like the other person. In this way alone can you outwit nature, which only requires you to perform copulation, and then to go out hunting for food. If you're going to play with affinities, you must use caution, you must secure a common ground for friendship!

I had my application packets in my pack. I requested Barry's appraisal. He looked them over one by one, digesting their information and promotional descriptions.

—I really do recommend the traditional route, he told me. This one's by far the best school around, he said, holding up the pamphlet of choice. It's run by Jesuits. I don't know how many Jesuits are teaching in the philosophy department, but I'm sure they're in control of it.

—That was my choice.

—I think it's important to have a traditional background, he said. You can always take it from there. If you transfer with the intention of studying philosophy, and of course you ought to make that known to them, they'll almost surely admit you.

I thanked him, and I eased back into my chair.

—So are you through for the day? he asked. Would you like to come over and check out my library? I have a pretty adequate collection. I'm really proud of it. I'm just a few blocks away.

At once I had my coat on. I zipped up my pack and we were on our way. And I too had something of a library, that is I held onto what my father had left to me. Something over a thousand volumes. Some excellent encyclopaedias and historical works—I had all of Durant and Toynbee and Spengler. My father majored in history at college, and history was always his hobby. And then of course I had the books I had accumulated on my own, a lifetime of school books—all the required texts and reading materials, and then some music history and lots of music methodology, those annoying sight-singing *solfeggio* manuals, and too many scores for piano. My baby grand has since become another book shelf. And I of course had all of Shakespeare, and loads of *companions* for the plays. I had a decent collection of science-fiction and horror paperbacks, too. Although I now think I devoted an inordinate amount of energy to consuming these—I read all the *Dune* books twice and I still don't figure how you *fold space,* although I think it's something akin to Cubism.

Barry's father was a doctor, a surgeon at New York Eye and Ear. His parents owned two adjoining apartments in this old apartment building on First at 74th. He said the building was now recognized by the Landmarks Preservation Commission. And indeed the entire façade had been meticulously restored. It was something right out of Edith Wharton. His living room—or, *the parlor,* as he called it—had this wrap-around balcony with a view of the East River. Stepping into Barry's home was like passing back in time to Old World Vienna. The place was crammed with antiques, and these were heirlooms, now, passed on from generation to generation. We had nothing like this in my family, or if we did, no one was telling *me* about it. There were glass cabinets displaying the most exquisite sculptured figurines, and between these cabinets, on pedestals, stood these brilliant and bizarre objects of modern sculpture. And they owned a Klimt, the most spellbinding Klimt I ever saw. They had a Steinway baby grand, and beside it was a cello. The cello was just resting there, as though someone had just finished playing.

He offered me a beverage and then led me to this hallway, this *gallery* of photographs that was right outside his bedroom. These were family portraits going back through the years to way before he was born. Most of them had been taken in Europe, around the time of the first World War. Some were taken outside a mansion on what seemed to be a great estate, and many were taken during picnics, in summertime, at this lake which I imagined was somewhere on the estate. I learned that Barry's father was born on this estate, and I learned that his grandparents, on both sides, were lost in the Holocaust. He would not say too much about this, and I thought it best not to question him, lest I should seem impolite. But then he pointed to a child in a photograph, and told me this was his paternal grandfather.

—This can horrify me, he said. When it catches me off guard. *All of this.* I try to stay awake to it. When it starts to seem like a dream, that's when it becomes unreal, and that's when it becomes mythology.

He then gestured and invited me to enter his room, which was indeed more of a library than just a bedroom. I suppose it is the case for many an introspective young in-tellectual, that the bedroom becomes his sanctuary, it's his study, his retreat, the space wherein he can most confidently realize his sensibilities. I was fortunate, I suppose, to have had my own apartment from a relatively young age. We never let go of my father's Manhattan apartment, which he owned and which I now own all to myself. Circumstances soon enough reached the stage where I was living on my own, for all practical purposes, with Aunt Gloria coming by regularly, if not daily, to see to my concerns. By the time I was sixteen, I was, for all practical purposes, living on my own, or, rather, living *it* alone. It was necessary, in our case. It sort of kept us all from murdering one another. It was a necessary distance. My cousins and I, we all reached adolescence at the same time, and then soon enough was the occasion, someone suggested I go occupy my *real* home. I suppose I was a lot of trouble, growing up. But when I was alone—and I know, 'cause I remember clearly—when I was alone I was a quiet child, and that's because I was always thinking, and talking to myself.

I noticed Barry too was in the habit of saving his school books, he had one entire bookcase reserved for their safe-keeping. It was excruciatingly apparent the amount of time and patience he had put into collecting, and keeping, his books. He had even begun to catalogue them on his compoohter.

—And they're cross-referenced, too. See? he said, then summoning up some sample data. But I'm steadily losing my faith in information, he said.

I watched the screen. It seemed he was compiling a general index for his entire collection. *I could never do this,* I thought.

—So what's left, then, when information's gone? I asked.

—The gut. I guess.

Meanwhile the contents of his index kept on scrolling past.

—So culture begins, I instigated, when the requirements of sex and food are met?

—*Are satisfied.* Culture *is* sex and food! *Solomon of old had a thousand concubines.* Culture begins at the time when sex moves from being a strictly procreative, strictly instinctual, unacquired, and therefore unconscious mode of response, to being an act performed strictly out of the conscious pursuit of pleasure, *or diversion.* Procreative sex became recreative sex when *sex* became too readily available, or so available that it became routine, and monotonous. Too many women, perhaps. *And the same goes for food.*

According to Barry, it was also at this time that *history* began, that is that man began to meditate on the phenomenon of death and the idea of eternity was born, and so too, then, the concepts of past, present, and future.

He was standing close beside me, staring straight into the screen, and looking sort of entranced. He had a peculiar expression on his face, not exactly smiling but more as though he were attempting to suppress his smile. And then something just crept up on me, a sort of tickly impulsiveness. I was smiling and my lips then felt the way they do when they're chapped, and they were parted as though I had something to say, only, I didn't have anything to say. I took a deep breath through my nose and I let it out slowly. He then did just the same. And now I was definitely nervous, though not as though I sensed a danger or felt threatened in any way, rather I felt as though I were about to run a track meet. I suppose I had that feeling like when I used to play hooky—I begin to tremble, first in my gut then straight into my knees and right back up into my gut again. It was a sort of not-altogether-disconcerting primordial anxiousness. And I thought, *this is just like playing hooky.* I tried to remain still, and I wondered if it showed. And I noticed he too was looking a bit peculiar himself.

—You are an interesting person to know, he said at last. I hope we remain friends a long time.

—Your nose, I began. Did they hurt you?

"The Guido Boys"

Joey Guido had this nervous energy condition in his face, his jaws were constantly in motion, chomping up and down, restlessly gnashing his molars. We all made believe we didn't notice it but as kids are wont to fix upon one another's afflictions and make of them descriptive handles and all it was inevitable that Joey would in no time come to be known as *Joey Jaws*. The popular psychology had it that Joey was caught in the act of masturbating and the jaws action was some sort of self-administered contrition. Catholic boys, you know, are dearly aware—if not *haunted*—by their shortcomings. The post-naughty-boy-guilt-stress-factor makes of all a heaven or hell predicament. As for myself I always believed that if you don't get caught you may as well just forget about it. This is the lie-and-deny tack. Of course if God really is omniscient then we don't stand a chance, in which case there's always the confessional, I suppose.

After school one day Joey snuck out his air rifle and commenced with the birds in the trees. The skittish ones were startled off by the puffs, but then this one rather hardy starling with a big oily head wouldn't so much as budge. Joey aimed and fired and clipped its wing. His brother Tommy hollered, *What the fuck ya doin'!* But Joey was having himself a fit. There was no way stopping him. The bird fluttered down into the gutter. Joey stood right on top of the thing, severing off its head. It took about a hundred pellets.

The Guidos owned a restored townhouse just a block south of Sutton Place. Father Guido owned a construction company. He built high-rise apartment buildings. The Guidos bought a new blue Wagoneer every two years, but that was just for the family, father Guido had himself a black Mercedes-Benz, with gold trim. On Saturdays Joey accompanied his father to the work site. He was being introduced into the business. Mother Guido was very strict with her boys, if one of them said anything critical or disparaging about somebody, she'd reprimand him on the spot. Once while we were watching TV in their basement, Joey remarked that the singer looked like she had breast implants. Mother Guido heard him from her kitchen. She came down and smacked him on the head. That evening Joey ran away, he said he was fed up with her riding him all the time. He came to my apartment with his sleeping bag. In the morning mother Guido rang the buzzer. She made us breakfast and she did all the dishes. Then Tommy came over and we all wound up at the Central Park zoo. Joey remarked that the gorilla looked like one of the janitors at school and mother Guido smacked him on the head for it. When Tommy got cancer and lost his leg, mother Guido gave him marijuana. It helped him with the chemotherapy.

My first real fist fight was with Joey Guido. It happened on Christmas Eve, during midnight Mass at St. Patrick's Cathedral. See, Tommy was a confirmed Mets fan and he wore his Mets cap religiously, even during the winter. He had his Mets cap on and Joey insisted that he remove it saying it was some sort of sacrilegious to wear a baseball cap in church. Tommy said he was praying for the Mets, and that the cap was his way of showing God that he meant it. Joey smacked him on the head and knocked it off. Now I was seated between them and as Joey did this his arm sort of rubbed against my nose, and as I always had a cold during Christmas some of my snot rubbed off onto his sleeve. Tommy said, *There, it's good for you!* And Joey, this time from behind me, smacked him on the head again. Tommy told him to lay off, and I said yeah, leave him be! Joey said Child, shut up and wipe your nose! I said you're just like your mother, riding him all the time! Then Joey got this stunned expression on his face and proceeded to pummel me right there in the pew. Hey! I said, just wait 'til I get you outside! By the end of the Mass I wasn't angry anymore, but Joey was secretly fuming. The second we got to the outside doors he proceeded to pummel on my head. Tommy, prosthesis and all, jumped him from behind and rolled with him down the steps. This was going on in front of everybody. They said take it across the street as though they didn't mind us fighting just don't do it on the steps of St. Patrick's, for Chrissake. I managed to get my balance and as Joey had by now thrown Tommy off we proceeded to exchange punches to the face. My nose was gushing snot and blood. Joey was bleeding from his ear. I don't recall throwing punches at his ears but as these things go you take what you can get. Then Joey somehow had me in a headlock and was doing this wrestling move he saw on TV. I was amazed at how strong he had become. I suppose it was from all that lifting he was doing every Saturday at the work site. He managed to get me into an abominable backbreaker hold and was about to smash me down when Tommy landed one straight for his solar plexus. That knocked the wind out of him. Then Mr. and Mrs. Guido made it over to us and Joey caught a smack on the head.

Now Joey's in the construction business. We still call him *Joey Jaws* when we talk about him but we don't call him it to his face anymore. Tommy got real sick and we called on him every day while he was in the hospital. He died on Joey's birthday. I've never been to Joey's office, but I hear he has a fresh bouquet of flowers on his desk every morning.

Reflecting on what Lydia said, *angels of God coupled with Uzi submachine guns,* I began a list of submachine gun parts.

Front sight
Barrel
Breech

—Stephen? she applies. She is doodling, doodling *Lydia* in precise vertical columns alternating in cursive and print. Did I tell you how I once saw my Uncle Jack's penis? *But really!* And now she is tracing her hand, tracing the outline of her hand over the columns reading *Lydia.* And it occurs to me that as a child that was how I used to draw my turkeys.

Rear sight

—This was at the time they were building their garden at the old Cos Cob house, and all those old, dead trees were up-rooted. *But of course you weren't there so that means nothing to you.*

Wind gauge
Stock

—I was playing around the side of the house, collecting pebbles for my wampum belt, and I wandered into the back. There was no one watching me. No one else outside, except for Uncle Jack.

Pistol grip
Trigger

—He was standing with his back to the path, and I, in my child-drowse, wandered up to him.

Magazine
Hand grip

—I guess he had just finished his business because he still held it in his hand. When he realized I was standing there beside him he didn't startle or become annoyed but rather casually asked if he could then see mine. I casually shook my head no. I remember replying so because I was thinking, I don't have one. *I hadn't one to show.* Looking back on it, however, rather would I have replied, *Certainly, meet Hypatia!* That Christmas he gave me the three-speeder.

Compensator
Sling

—I remember, there occurred a rash of burglaries around the neighborhood. There were rumors circulating at school as to who was committing the reckless break-ins. It was Ken, who used to play baseball with a cigarette dangling in his mouth, and his kid brother, Rob, who everyone thought was a dwarf until his fourteenth year when he sprang up six inches. These two, their parents belonged to the Society of Friends. Ken and Rob Henley knew who was away on vacation or out golfing or playing tennis at the club because the homes they were robbing belonged to their friends. Well, following upon the rumors, these two detectives invaded the neighborhood, grilling all the kids for information. I came home from class to find them waiting in the living room. They were seated on the old davenport, my mother was serving them iced tea. I remember she seemed especially ridiculously reticent and fainthearted, yielding to the detectives' ordering me into a chair then turning her back and withdrawing to her kitchen. I remember having to pee so badly, and asking to be momentarily excused. The one detective turned to the other, then turned back to me, saying, *so you can warn your accomplices?* I was mortified. We spoke to everyone, they said. *We know everything!* I looked over my shoulder for my mother, and damn if she wasn't gone! She left me there. *A fifteen-year-old girl!* With these two fucking stiffs. I'll never forget how one of them, pulling up on his waist-band and resting his palm on the heel of his revolver, asked, *are you having sex with these boys?* I was mortified. *That these two working-class white-trasher stiffs should ask me such a question!* I mean, *look at me!* I'm blond. I'm svelte. I'm a *WASP. I'm a fucking national treasure!* And when I was fifteen I was what those fucking stiffs were all about protecting! And I hated her for leaving me alone with them.

She is light upon my bed, her legs are crossed in Lotus posture, *shalom posture,* she calls it. And I am at my desk, doodling a list, doodling my name in precise vertical columns alternating in cursive and print. Outwardly, she is silent, unmoving, withheld. But inwardly there rages, there rages. *A debate!* As to which plea to enter.

I am her chorus. . . .

Everything is wrong, but you.

The tears are ready, and willing to comply. Are these, at last, the tears of the merely maladjusted, more symptom, sign of what she's yet to bring to light? Or are they, *Ave Marie,* a final curtain call. *Good-bye to all that!*

Everything is wrong, but you.

—I must grasp this station I now occupy as far removed from that of my childhood.

And I think, *oh, my Lydia, easier said than done.*

I leave my desk to rest my head upon her lap, for I, at last, am the glutton. The taste of her tear is as a water of life. And Aphrodite, she was borne of the sea. And Odysseus, he forever did merge the taste of the sea to the weeping-song of a Siren.

Everything is wrong, but you!

—Rub my feet! she commands, unshaloming her legs. *Put pressure where the spike went through His foot.*
—What can I do for you?
—Make a list!

Pumps.
Spectators.
Oxfords.
Ghillies.
Mules.
Slingbacks.

—It's not doin' it fer me.

The Chosen People.
The Sermon on the Mount.
The Communist Manifesto.
Social Realism.
Andy Warhol.

—*Basta!* I want a hungry list.

First and foremost, strong wine.
Sweet dark port.
Then vegetables.

Beans.
Asparagus and Brussels sprouts.
Fresh broccoli,
steamed, and chilled and served with lemon juice,
and plenty of pressed garlic, and salt and coarse black pepper.
Roots of every sort,
well seasoned and with plenty of white pepper.
Garden radishes.
Lettuces.
Endive.
Leeks.
Onions.
Pine-nuts.
Pistachios.
Sweet almonds.
Syrups.
Nectars.
Snails. The escargot.
Candied citrons.
Shell-fish.
Soft shell crabs.
And shrimp and lobster. Lobsters Newburg and thermidor.
Jambalaya.
Blackened, for Chrissake, red and blue

—One fish, two.

Poultry.
Chicken. Chicken gumbo.
Game.
We'll see the game menu, please.
Testicle of bull.

> *Hard-boiled eggs.*
> *Nouvelle sauces.*
> *Choice fruits.*
> *Bananas.*
> *No! No bananas, bananas make you sleepy.*

—Really. As in, it makes perfect sense the people who eat tropical fruit are the *siesta* people.

> *We are what we eat.*
> *Cakes.*
> *Puddings and tarts.*
> *Scents.*
> *Soft light.*
> *Candlelight.*
> *Soft pillows and covers and couches and ottomans.*
> *And what's-his-name, divine on the divan.*
> *Still hungry?*

—For Chrissake, Stephen. The reason she couldn't defend me was because she was drunk. *Drunkity, drunkity, drunkity.* Every afternoon, when I'd come home from class. Or I would find her in her sewing room, flat on her back on the day bed. And I knew the world was spinning inside that head. She'd look up at me, and smile, and say, *hungry? Did you eat your lunch?* And I asked, what's bothering you, Mom? And she'd say, *Oh, Lydia. What have I done to myself?* And begin the whole self-pity routine. And that's what really made me disgusted. She got all sloppy and wishy-washy and weak. And I just couldn't love her anymore. I needed her to be strong. Tell me, Stephen, do you ever recall your Christmases past? Are you wont to summon such memories? *Or are you sane!*

I do not answer, not exactly, but rather sigh an abounding sigh.

Everything is wrong, but you.

—I'm thinking, now, of how our adorable little Nativity scene did once so utterly and conspicuously disappear from beneath our tree. And how it did then reappear, *but just in time for your arrival.* For years it was stuffed inside its crush-proof box, hidden away behind all that junk in the attic. And we all knew it was there. We all knew its location exactly. No one until your arrival, no one until I and out of shame thinking what you would think thought to fix the incongruity. In spite of the fact that we all knew privately the same humiliation. *We all knew what was missing.* No one felt the necessity enough to dig it out and bring it down. But then it's not the sort of impulse one is wont to act upon. No, it's not like the impulse to shout and to accuse, to hit where it hurts and to deny. It's not a thing of immediate gratification. *Oh! The idea! To hit where it hurts! To injure our loved ones.* Well, nothing like a little incentive. She removed it because she had a bad conscience. She felt guilty, being a drunken lush and all. Now she's got all these lines and wrinkles. And I can no longer look into her eyes. *I have forgotten the color of my mother's eyes.* And she can't even write her name any more. Her handwriting is illegible. Which somehow brings to mind, and talk about a nonentity, where oh where has my big brother gone? And what wonder how none of this has fazed him. Real men don't dance, you see. Not with their little sisters. He's the strong, silent type. He won't show his emotions. He'd rather not discuss it. *I tell you my brother is a stranger to me.* Now granted, I could, should you press me, pick him out of a midtown crowd. But as to what is going on inside the man? I'm a blank. He's very surface-oriented, you see, very concerned about his image, which is why he'll have nothing to do with me. I'm a dangerous situation, a problem just waiting to surface. I'm too unpredictable. I'm liable to ask the wrong question, bring up the wrong subject and wrinkle his *façade.* I might ask, *do you remember when Mommy?* Or, *come to think of it, isn't Daddy weak?* I'm too unpredictable. He can't control me so he'll have nothing to do with me. No resolutions. Just abrupt and *quiet-if-you-please* conclusions. The years hurry by, we mature into adulthood, and suddenly it strikes us, as it most churlishly has stricken me, that we have failed to establish a sincere and candid rapport. So in a very real sense my brother and I are strangers. Now yes, we have established our means of skirting about the edges of each other, we have our prejudicial rallying points, you might say, but generally, and most importantly, it seems, we have philosophical and world-view taboos, points and opinions and attitudes which once uncovered cannot but send us scurrying into opposing corners. I know this is true in most families, I'm aware of that, and regardless of whether the mother's a lush, and much of it is sibling rivalry, but those who hang on the sibling rivalry angle are not dipping beneath the surface, as sibling rivalry must eventually give sway to openhearted accommodation, or else it ossifies, it obdurates, it settles in the soul and one grows ever so accustomed. Yet maybe it only seems this way, that is maybe I'm exaggerating too much into my understanding of our estrangement, of *my* estrangement, anyway, because, you know, he seems perfectly willing to carry on as though the entire situation were just peachy, as though this is the way things ought to be between us, as though we could not or should not hope for or strive to achieve any better understanding. *But is it me?* I cannot ignore my reading of these things, for *I* do not go scurrying off into my corner, rather do I remain, center ring, imagination and sympathy intact. *Imagination plus sympathy equals empathy.* He seems perfectly comfortable and indeed satisfied to hold as valid his adolescent, his outdated and obsolete observations and formulations as to what exactly constitutes my attitude. He is somehow unable or unwilling to adjust. My proposals, my comments, my input, these he cannot but construe to be antagonisms. I have no credibility at all with him. It is as it is with my parents. *I have no credibility!* Meanwhile I'm left holding my finger in the dike! *Now please let go of my foot!*

Ach, du!

Barry never failed to crack me up. And he was right-on dead pan, every time. Discussing food and sex, *our topics of decision,* he said wherever you encounter good food there too you're likely to encounter good sex. Or something to that effect.

—Take France, and the Italians, he told. No wonder what ails England and the U.S. Good cuisine is an indication of good sex. I'm talking quality, now, not quantity. And over pop-ulation is not so much an indication of good food, or of good sex, so much as it may indicate a lack of creativity. *I wonder what ate Malthus and Ricardo?* But Stephen, *can you smell it? The revolt of the burger and fries!*

He told me these things as though they were the gospel truth. And I think he was convinced, or else I was convinced of his conviction. The way he said them, with such passion and conviction. And then so terribly disappointed—disappointed by the prospect that perhaps it was all true. Barry wants to build upon the ruins, build upon the deconstructed ruins, but as a child at play amid the rubble of a South Bronx lot. *Castles out of broken glass.*

My face is too serious. I am too young to be of such serious
face. Daily would I check my face in mirrors, in windows, in
puddles. On hand and knee I hovered over puddles. . . .

"Auto the Vampire"

I have never seen the sunrise. I have read descriptions of the dawn, and of noon and of dusk,
seen from mountaintop, valley and shore. I have
collected French paintings, and drawings and photographs, from the world over, of the drama of the
sunlight.
—But how you clasp your hands. It is absurdly
mimetic of prayer.
—Yes. I know that, now.
—I was watching from above.
—You are a beautiful woman.
—And you, a hungry man.
—Not a man. A beast. *A hungry beast.*
—And I a marble sasin, *on which you crack your*
teeth.

Christ! What've I done? I backed out of my own graduation! Three
years at the goddam place and I couldn't stand to attend my

own graduation. And my picture won't appear in the yearbook. No neat account of my activities.

*You must not allow yourself to become discouraged.
Your true mettle lies in perseverance.*

How did she know? How *could* she know! *Imagine my chagrin.*

And so I did enroll at the Jesuit university. My plan was to stay on for two years, for the bachelor's in philosophy, I would then either remain or move on to *who knows where* for the graduate courses. I was intent on devoting the next years of my life to the study of philosophy. And really, I had no more-productive alternative. I would not need to secure an income. It's not like I'm rich or anything. I'm not *rich.* I'm more a victim of circumstances. One thing for sure about my father, he was a massive believer in insurance policies. He left me more than financially able. Still, it's meager compensation, were it not for my Aunt Gloria.

But I still had doubts as to whether college was the place to be. While I knew that I could benefit by the structure of an academic setting, and that I needed to learn the principles of my subject, indeed the principles of philosophical study, I also knew that the knowledge I was after could not be found in any academic textbook, or in a classroom setting. All this was a divergence from the real work to be done, the real knowledge to be gained. And there remained some sticky conflicts that I'd yet to find the answers for, such as the bad conscience I was shouldering for all that PC dogma crap at that paper, and then this namby-pamby, affectedly nice and dictaphobic disposition that seems to have infected everybody except myself. I had the unwelcome sense that my professors had in a manner gone *belly up,* and were more concerned with the success of their own careers, which for all practical purposes meant upholding the PC line, and being namby-pamby and affectedly nice and dictaphobic. I had the unwelcome sense that it was *this,* that it was not for informing us impartially, especially where historical *fact* gave room for opinionated interpretation. The journalism courses I'd taken seemed geared to make of us left-wing guerrilla muckrakers. In class, discussion of news issues and events was paramount, but not with the aim of *how* to think, it was more about *what* to think, *and then who to think it for.* Technical procedures and methods—the correction and development of such—was secondary, *but so as to seem nonessential.* I could not shake the thought of impudent children taking liberties off inordinately permissive adults. *Yes, but where were the adults?* At other times it seemed the product of a downright pathological envy. One day in class I made a fool of myself, I raised my hand and said, *in a perfect world there are no inferiority complexes, there is no class envy, there is no race envy.* No one looked at me or said a word. The professor looked at me as though I were Beelzebub himself.

The flesh-colored prosthesis
Bone loss after menopause
A German-speaking Japanese
A Japanese in blackface
Yoko Ono
The klezmer yippie
The Maharishi Spite
War crimes
The hero dog

Gregory Vincent St. Thomasino

The soccer match stampede
The paper napkin
Key pad
I-beam
Thong bikini

I waited out the summer immersed in some books Barry had listed for me, they were a dictionary of philosophers and philosophical terms and trends, another and less wordy dictionary of philosophers and philosophical terms and trends, W.K.C. Guthrie's *The Greek Philosophers,* Philip Wheelwright's *The Presocratics,* volume three of Werner Jaeger's *Paideia,* and then the first volume in Frederick Copleston's *A History of Philosophy.* Either owing to Barry's list, or perhaps these coupled with my earnestness, the result of my readings was time and again to urge my interests further on. I gained a fresh appreciation for my own books, especially the Durant set. I now wanted nothing less than to read and *learn* the authors and trends of Western philosophy—*but indeed of Western civilization!* And I was possessed of the romantic notion of studying at the university and of having my earnestness, *my inspiration and my sincerity,* greeted and nurtured by the same.

My correspondence with Susanna was constant as ever but our words showed signs of diverging paths, she would not pick up on my telling of my new friend Barry, or even on my mention of my studies, and she made mention of a young man she had by now grown loyal to, most of all we did not meet that August, in spite of what we had planned. And dauntless Barry was gone for Israel, he abandoned his plans for NYU and was off to study classics with a renowned professor he'd been writing to and hoping to study with. He took along some of his library—two big trunks, and then some. I helped him box up his computer. I can imagine him garreted in his apartment in Jerusalem with the buzzer disconnected. I can imagine him marrying an intense young Jewish woman with a mythologically beautiful face. There are such women who fall for studious young men. Lydia's Dr. Freud sure seemed to be a studious sort of fellow, only he was not so young. It was a while since I'd last seen her, disappearing into that townhouse. Sometimes I thought of hiking up there and staking out the place with the notion of spying on her. Well, not really *to spy,* but perhaps just to see her a little, to see if maybe she had changed, like changed her hair or her style of clothes. In any case, these were not the points of our affinity, *style of dress or of appearance.* What we shared was a beauty, a psychology, an inner association and philosophical camaraderie. There's no more precise or accessible way of putting it. We discussed it often enough. We considered ourselves two peas in a pod. It was *her* expression. *Petits pois.*

Lydia is terribly typically middle-class. She once described herself as *a logger-brained, middle-classified malcontent.* Which of course explains her Ph.D.

—There is just so much to un-do, she stated, and so emphatically and on more than one occasion. We are sentenced, this is our affliction, to wallow in the puddle of our parents' delusions plashed curb-side at Main. But of course, you don't have this problem.

—Not exactly.

—It is said, by no means is it easy for those to rise from obscurity whose noble, *noble!* Now there's a term can send a middle-classer into an irrecoverable tailspin! Whose *noble* qualities are hindered by straitened circumstances at home. This is the classic struggle of one's aspirations with one's circumstances.

Why just the mention of religion, of art or of literature, is enough to send a middle-classer into an irrecoverable tailspin. Just the mention of religion, of art or of literature is enough to clear the air of all munificence!

And really, I suppose, this was our second strongest bond, sharing this most loathsome fact of our existence. *Being and hating to be products of the middle-class mentality and character.* We felt we lacked the dignity and elevation of character, *the freedom and poise,* of the old and more often than not eccentric aristocrats we read about in our novels and chose to believe actually existed. We felt elevation of character didn't cost anything but the sloughing off of old, involuntary ways and the acquiring, by moral effort, of new, intentional ones, while at the same time we lacked the righteous indignation of the politically newly arrived and empowered minorities who were forever hoisting new demands in an increasingly combative chorus of voice. We were in the middle, the undignified and commonplace and virtually nondescript middle, and we supposedly had nothing to complain about. But we knew we were moralistically bankrupt. We knew neither money nor social status nor political influence could replenish our enervated stores. And we felt wonder and surprise at the ever obvious certainty that the insulated rich as well as the deference demanding minorities had no real clue as to the force and breadth of our dissent.

—I declare this unsalvable mediocrity a pestilent rift in the continuity of our heritage! she protested.

We termed our age and generation, the *Meat Epoch.* Because we lacked a metaphysics. And we were *passive blank.* Because we, meaning *them,* had neither the stuff nor the inclination to generate new values. It was a matter of moral inertia. And we took on as our fate to be soldiers in this metaphysical and cultural war of attrition. We would be the creators of a new intellectual tradition. And we held our sensibilities and imaginations to a height where no mere cynicism can apply. And we swore these ideals did far extend beyond our love and our relationship. Together or apart, together *and* apart, we both had something to strive for.

—There is a war taking place, she told, and we are in the midst of it! It is a campaign to annul our heritage and the values which therefrom do constitute the very stuff of our psyches. And what is it at stake? *Everything we have to live for!*

So really, I suppose, we were not exactly at zero. All things, still, were not of equal value. The poet, the artist, the philosopher, and the priest and the astronaut, even, because they explored the frontiers of the intellectual, the reflective, and of the symbolical, of the imaginative and the intuitive, the realms of intention and extension, for these reasons they were in themselves encouraging and promising of the force that would act upon our moral inertia. We had only to expose ourselves, in a manner at once resolute and open-minded, to their influence. *Our* frontier was as obvious as any other, and perhaps even more so. The Apocalypse had indeed occurred, only, we had slept ourselves through it. And our frontier—*no fecund Canaan, this, but a famine wasteland!*—lay before us, indeed *within our hearts and minds.* For behind the thought that humankind was now capable of *physical* annihilation, via *the bomb,* hides the more and immediate truth that we have already annihilated ourselves, via our philosophy, *metaphysically. For sure, Man still had possession of his brain, but somewhere along the line, circa 1968, he had willingly surrendered his mind.*

I shared all this with Barry, and I was not surprised to learn that he had reached the same conclusions.

—We have interpreted away all the gnosis, he added, and as something of a lamentation. This is problematical. But then this is also a call for creativity. We acknowledge the quasi-absolutism of the law, *quasi* because laws are subject to change. This aspect of the law is the bond that holds us to our legal agreements. We could not conduct ourselves as businessmen and legislators without it. But morally, it seems, and given to cultural relativism and contextualism, morally, we are lost in space. We are rudderless. Scripture is open to question. Indeed so are *all* our value signs, except perhaps the omnipotent dollar sign, everyone seems to agree upon *that* efficacy, everyone except the anarchists, that is, *but then they don't even believe in soap.* You know, I never knew an anarchist who was capable of dialectical thinking. It will be interesting to see which *will to power* captures control and dominates the field. For the time being, the vulgarians hold sway. For the time being, at least, our moral futures are up for grabs. So tell me, Stephen, *shall we sit idly by while others determine our values? Shall we live like shy deer, hidden in the woods?*

I wanted so much to revive this discussion with Lydia, *or even with Susanna,* but I knew that that was impossible now. To invade her space would mean to violate our trust, and at last forfeit my credibility. And besides, did I even know her whereabouts? My thoughts of her were this *fusion* of recollection and projection, and at last, *alas,* impulsive presumptuousness.

And so I did enroll at the Jesuit university. . . .

It was part freshman orientation, part training in social awareness, and part, methinks, like being searched for lice, this, *sensitivity awareness seminar,* a pretty recent phenomenon universities all over were adopting as part of their first term requirements for all newly admitted students. I had up to this time been immune to such things, such things as *neo-social indoctrination,* but now, being as I was enrolled at a college of indisputable renown, and being as my overall state of mind was such that hopefulness held sway, I accepted it, this prod at my rump, in à la the passive acquiescence. They had accepted all of my credits, so I was set so far as concerned the core requirements, but everyone was *to that which must be done* the sensitivity credits, absolutely no waivers were granted, and not that I would have applied for one, nix this sort of official *mixer* thing, but three credits at *$280* per had me thinking whether I could not acquit my misanthropy. This seminar-style, three-hour *course,* christened, Human Resources Institute, met once a week. The director was one Father Francis Dunn, *Society of Jesus.* I took to Father Dunn almost immediately, because, well, at our first meeting I was sort of giving him the once-over, sort of sizing him up to determine whether he had a spine in there somewhere, and he sort of got the drift of my expression, and instead of going all defensive on me he sort of made this face of resignation and rolled his eyes *upward* as though to say *uh-oh, I got a live one here,* and I sort of found that endearing. Besides, *Francis* is a righteous name. And his middle initial was *X.*

So Father Dunn explained how we all were there for no reason other than that it seemed a good idea and that it seemed to be working out all right so far. He said that should any of us have an idea about an issue or current event or article or editorial or book or film that we might wish to discuss then by all means feel free to bring it up. He filled us in on all the clubs on campus and the papers and the journals and the upcoming retreats that we might wish to take part in. He gave out a list of Websites and phone numbers—I could never resist a good list—and maps of the campus and a whole lot of getting acquainted material, and then began a history of the athletics department and on all the teams and how they were doing in the standings. I felt sort of silly and juvenile for all this, and I thought of Lydia teaching class at Columbia, and having sex with this sixty-year-old man, and I wanted to cringe with humiliation, in fact I did cringe a little but then I caught myself lest Father Dunn think I was cringing for him. Father Dunn really beamed when he spoke about athletics, this was obviously a major source of pride and enjoyment for him. He carried on about the teams for the better part of the meeting. I sat there, battling my impulsiveness, trying not to lose control of my imagination. I wanted to get on to some serious discussion of the problem of our moral inertia, but as I stealthily looked around at the other students I saw how they were smiling and enjoying themselves and really getting into Father Dunn's presentation, and, oddly, a wave of relief came over me. And besides, Father Dunn had by now unveiled his team cap, and somebody called out, *put it on!*

My whole summer's reading was in effect a preparation, a *propaedeutic,* for my class in ancient Greek philosophy. I was, to say the least, revved up. My professor, however, was long beyond any such ebullience.

Professor Mary Agnes O'Gallagher. Right down to her blue imitation-leather gum-soles and matching purse that snapped shut. And when she wrote on the board, and when she wrote on the board only her wrist and forearm moved, her hips remained stiff. *'Tis a miracle,* I wondered, when she said she had five daughters, and I almost said out loud, *I don't believe you!* She gave me the impression that she was suspicious of me, and I could not fathom why, except that maybe it was because

I had my copies of Copleston and Wheelwright on my desk, and maybe these gave her the impression that I was already up on things, and that maybe I might be straining her, or judging her. She reminded me of one of those old blue-haired ewes you used to find behind the registers at Woolworth's. Suspicious, edgy, get-too-close-the-smell'll-stain-ya sort of boy-hating old ewes. There was this one Halloween, I met my classmate Bobby "the straightedge" Allison and we were cruising the Woolworth's on 86th. We were checking out their Halloween aisle. We wanted wigs but their old-witch's wigs were really cheap and bogus-looking. So we thought *hey, why not check out the real wigs, the ones they sell all year round!* So that's what we were up to when this blue-haired powder puss sneaks up behind us and all but frightens us out of our pants. She accused us of planning to swipe the damn thing. *Like for Chrissake.* I pulled out my cash and counted out some bucks saying *see, we can purchase whatever we like.* And I asked her, please, to apologize. Instead she kept on bird dogging us 'til we were clear out onto the sidewalk. And then she stood by the doors with this tight-lipped expression, arms folded at her chest. Her mind was all made up.

So Dr. Mary Agnes O'Gallagher, by way of *beans* and the Pythagorean brotherhood, starts off on this bender over health food. *Salame, bologna, kielbasi, pepperoni, white bread.* . . . I morphed into something sluglike, hoping not to be too obvious.

"Que sçais je?"

The monks of Fossanuova, after St. Thomas
Aquinas had died in their monastery and in their fear
of losing the relic, did not shrink from decapitating,
boiling and preserving the body.

During the lying in state of St. Elizabeth of Hungary, a crowd of worshippers came and tore strips of the linen covering her face. They cut off her hair, her nails, and her nipples, even.

King Charles VI of France, on the occasion of a solemn feast, distributed the ribs of his ancestor, St. Louis. To Pierre d'Ailly and to his uncles Berry and Burgundy he gave entire ribs, and to the prelates he gave one bone to divide between them, which they proceeded to do after the meal.

At our next HRI meeting Father Dunn had us arrange our chairs into a circle. He remained standing at his lectern, outside our circle, at the head of the room. After everyone had settled down he asked that we begin by introducing ourselves. But there was something preoccupying him, his tone and manner were conspicuously changed, and this not only caught *my* attention, it impressed the others as well as we all settled down a bit too quickly. He seemed a bit too formal, a little priestly, even.

A woman's voice, sweet and charming, but then direct and none too light-minded-sounding, and in a short, pleated, schoolgirl skirt, brown saddle bucks and cardigan, and with a handsome tortoise-shell hair band, volunteered to start us off.

—Well, I'm *black,* as you can see. No, *I really am black!*

Her name was Michelle O'Garro. She was eighteen and was planning on Communications for her major. She said her grandparents were Baptists, but that her parents, because her mother was, were Catholic, and that she had always gone to Catholic schools. I was just about slipping into slug mode—aiming in part to figure Father Dunn's peculiar mood—when I picked up on her telling of the chore she had that morning managing a drop/add transfer. It was not the procedure itself, and all the traveling around they made her do, but what had her goat was the professor whose class she felt she needed to avoid.

—She stands before the class, with her cup of hot coffee, slurping between sentences, and you can smell her coffee-breath.

She clearly disapproved of the woman's delivery. She was describing her pretty thoroughly, with special emphasis on the way she gestures with the cup.

—And I'm waiting for the coffee to spill on my head.

She attended three meetings, she said. The distraction became too much for her. As she spoke she tried to attract the eyes of the others in our circle. It was disheartening, albeit not surprising, how everyone in turn shied away from making some sort of connection with her. But not even to the point of a sympathetic nod. And I felt how in a sense they were denying her the legitimacy of her frustration, they were denying her her credibility. This can be unbearably suffocating for someone who is genuinely and perhaps justifiably piqued. When at last she tried for *my* eyes I shook my head big nifty *yes. I thought someone ought to rally her spirits!* College freshmen, which for the most part made up our group, and for all their sheepishness, are reluctant to support such discontents, they are at this stage safely afield, it's all *impersonal* to them, and if only because they don't know if they like you yet.

I saw to Father Dunn at his lectern. He was still with the sober expression only now it bordered on solemnity. I wondered if perhaps this was his Mass face, and if so, *was it, perhaps, a funeral Mass? And had he baptized anyone lately?* Would he pick up on her telling and enlighten us as to some basic points of pedagogy? I did not expect him to defend the professor, nor to reckon aloud the frivolity of it. And yet I might have expected him to interject a thought or two. He turned to the door as though expecting an arrival, then his eyes returned to the lectern. He seemed in fact to be perusing something. I saw him raise a page up close to his eyes as though inspecting for a misprint or inaccuracy. Perhaps a word or sentence had him vexed and he was trying for a better understanding.

Michelle was finished soon enough, she concluded saying how on account of this professor she was now enrolled in an evening class. Some others took their turns at introducing themselves. I listened for some beefs. Everyone sort of followed suit with Michelle, but just to the extent where they told their names and their prospective majors and career goals. One guy, Ben McCarthy, in a pink Ralph Lauren oxford and baggy new jeans could not exactly *speak* his age, but sort of *belched* it out in two parts—*ate*-teen. This was truly remarkable. He was apparently well practiced. There's nothing like a healthy boyish belch. Methinks it to become fair etiquette. Ben was a big, beefy athletic boy, with fresh ruddy cheeks and an effortless smile. America's favorite son. And obviously a big-time passive-blanker, one of our color guard, for sure. The passive blank color guard is composed primarily of party animals. I can imagine Ben flattening beer cans on his forehead and dancing around in his briefs. He said he wanted to work at the Stock Exchange.

As for the make-up of our group, it was indicative of the entire student body. Aside from a few Filipinos, which is to be expected at a Jesuit school—the three in our group were out for psych majors, experimental as opposed to clinical, of course—and two or three not-yet-politicized neo-beatnik sorts, and with no obvious tattoos or piercings—I always thought of the whole neo-beatnik thing as a sort of conformism disguised as a non-conformism, and essentially just another form of consumerism—well, everyone seemed essentially middle-clas-sified, even the blacks. Here were squeaky-clean collegiates. Grist for the wheel. *Fattened for the table.* Bright-eyed and bushy-tailed and well adjusted, and preparing to take their rightful places as parents and workers and guardians of the almighty dollar sign. The girls, for the most part, all seemed to have or affected Connecticut accents, or else they spoke a sort of college-girl *I'm privileged* locution that reminded me of Lydia when we first met, only Lydia's diction—her choice of words and phraseology—so empowered it all that it carried the force of a martial sally. It's all in the inflections, the pitch or tone of voice. For instance, take the word, *home.* It's all in the huff on *ho,* and then a sort of hum or drone on the *ome.* Your ear gets used to it soon enough. I suppose it's charming. Sort of. Charming in a come-sit-on-your-daddy's-knee sort of way. These girls, they're all crazy for their fathers. They all get along famously. And some are crazy for their mothers—these are the sort that remain virgins way into their thirties. But here's what gave Lydia her edge, she dislikes her old man something fierce. She blames him for her mother's drinking. . . .

—He's a lawyer for a national insurance company. He challenges claims in court. And for all his Episcopalianisms he's adept as hell at denying compensations. Has about as much empathy as a landlord.

Father Dunn at last called a break. In a wink we were up and heading for the door. On the way I happened to detect Michelle's eye, it seemed she was looking to attract my atten-tion. I smiled and rolled my eyes a little, I wanted to express my relief for the break, and for the fact that I got away without having to introduce myself. She smiled and we met at the door. We walked down the hall together and came to a stop at the water fountain. The water fountain looked like it was a hundred years old and was beside this old glass firehose cabinet. The firehose looked like it had never been unraveled and had an antique brass nozzle.

—Do you believe how they keep this thing polished! I began.

—It's a private school, she replied, and seeming not at all impressed. They have the patience, she said. You made it safely out of there.

—I know. Maybe he'll make me go when we get back. It isn't fair to you or to the others.

—Don't do it if your heart isn't in it. Father Dunn won't mind. *I* won't mind.

—You know Father Dunn?

—I have him for my *Distinguished Lectures* course.

—I like him, I said.

—Father Dunn is a gentleman.

—Stephen Child, I said, putting out my hand.

—You already know *my* name.

—*Michelle.* Yes. I like your name.

We stood quietly a moment, just looking in the direction of the classroom. I was listening to the echo in the hallway, to the footsteps and the voices, and I thought I heard a clap of thunder and I thought I'll have to check to see if it's raining, and I was looking for our reflections on the glass when, suddenly, surprisingly, I met her eyes in the reflection. At once I thought to turn away, as I expected her to turn, but she didn't, and we just stood there, quietly, watching each other in our reflections on the glass. Two boys turned the corner rolling a TV into our room. Father Dunn motioned us back inside. We rearranged our chairs as he pushed a disc into the player. Michelle and I sat together now. He skipped introducing the program and took a seat next to Michelle. I noticed he was prepared to follow along with a transcript. *So that's what he was perusing!*

The program was of an interview with this Nobel Prize laureate. I had seen this author before. He's a Holocaust survivor. His books are terrifying and formidable accounts of the experiences he endured as a concentration camp prisoner. Certainly, I wondered, our whole group was familiar with his visage, if not his name.

—I've seen this man! I said. Marcel Greene. *On PBS.*

—I think I've seen this interview, said Michelle.

—*Marcel Greene,* said Father Dunn, aloud for all to hear. Now I have not seen this program, he continued. And we're short on time. Let's pay some attention.

The camera panned so to show the pair of crutches within the author's reach. His legs seemed to hang awkwardly, and then, at his ankles, just beneath his cuff, there showed a section of his leg brace.

He was slouched into his chair, clearly this could not be avoided, and it made him seem weary and dispirited, but then he raised his eyes and held his head as though his strength was all in his shoulders. This was not the face of an insouciant man, rather here was the face of a man of perseverance and persistence. There seemed an inexplicable loneliness about him. Are not these creases at his mouth the internalized strains of an heroic endurance, the unmistakable and undeniable, indelible imprint of a pain and distress that has forced its integration with his being. Yet there is nothing desolate about him, and rather are these creases as much the sign of an elegant smile and profound tenderness.

His accent is thick, probably Yiddish and French, but beyond this, in this voice at once resolute and yielding, I cannot help but discern an unhappy tentativeness. It is the tentativeness of one who must relate an unfathomable tale and is uncertain as to whether his audience is prepared to conceive and to comprehend. And I am made uneasy by this voice, for in this voice I can discern the timbre of the bedtime story.

—*Why?* he asks, and by his tone and by his eyes, the question is not wholly rhetorical. *Why did they do this to the Jews?*

Father Dunn really came out of left field with this, or else this was what these HRI meetings were all about. A sort of clinical confrontation, like it or not, with those elements of human nature that we've yet to overcome. The pathology of malevolence. The sort of things one is likely to encounter ordinarily.

The man is speaking now as though entranced. He speaks as though from within a trance. Is not retelling to some degree a reliving? And I wonder if he submits himself to hypnotherapy, because he seems, now and again, to slip into a deeper and deeper concentration, and during these brief moments his voice seems to take on that talking-in-one's-sleep sound. *Retelling is reliving.* I sort of know about this stuff because I underwent it for myself. There was a point during which I believed I had murdered my parents. For some time, a while ago, I truly believed I was responsible for my father's death, and I sort of kept it to myself as a secret. Anyway, I heard these tapes of myself talking it over, and I swear I hear him sounding so.

Retelling is reliving. And with each recreating does he not, perhaps, discover *more*, is not his consciousness increased? Does not this increase mean greater poignancy? Greater accuracy? And nuance? And perhaps it is his wish to strike an empathy into our *passive blank* consciousnesses. Or is it, *consciences?* And with this empathy, perhaps there will be introduced a shock of recognition that will deepen, widen, awaken a receptivity, a continuity. And with each *continuity* he does succeed to cast, his own consciousness, while it is not in the least bit assuaged, is, rather, *legitimized.*

And I think, *What can I do to lessen his injury?* And I think, *I can do nothing.* And I think, *What can I do to restore what has been wrenched from this man?* And I think, *I can do nothing.* And he says, above a tone, *but is it resignation. . . .*

—*So long as there are Catholics, catastrophes, there will be no peace for the Jews.*

And I turn to Father Dunn who is reading, re-reading this passage in the transcript. I look for his expression, and perhaps a response. And there is none, not immediately, but that same sober composure.

There was no time for a discussion period, at the close we all just pretty politely, courteously, *reverentially,* I think, upped and left the room. There was no sound of chairs squeaking against the floor, or of the usual sign-of-relief chatter, only the raindrops striking the windowpanes. Everyone, I think, was refraining from breathing. I know I was, but my mind, my thoughts and my emotions, I felt my heart beating in my chest.

Father Dunn remained behind, still perusing the transcript.

I read so much philosophy, that first year, that it was literally affecting my dreams. I would awaken at all hours of the night, and I would try to retrieve what I worried were these break-through articulations, reformulations of questions and impasses, but I was hardly ever able to preserve them, and then not in any usable or sensible form, before they scattered and were gone. It was an unwelcome feat, reaching for the lamp and opening my notebook, and then racking my brains trying to recollect the contents of my dream. And then I was up for the rest of the night, sleepless and unhappy, frustrated and disappointed, and it was not a dream, I considered, but a nightmare. What I did manage to scribble down was better suited for a poem than for a paper in philosophy. In my dream I could actually *know* the articulations, I could actually *feel* as though I were one with the concepts. I could *experience* a joy, a gratification, the gratification that accompanies comprehension, *but the comprehension of an unbounded web.*

In my letter to Barry that June I expressed my bafflement and fascination over this. He replied, *Congratulations!* And then he wrote that I was studying too hard. He wrote that in philosophy, the perennial problems are indeed resolved again and again, only not so much as by discovering or contriving enduring solutions, but rather by re-articulating, re-stating the perplexity in up-dated and contemporary terms. He thought that my dreams were probably an indication that the subject was within my reach. And he wrote that Francis Bacon had declared the Jesuits to be the best teachers that civilization had produced. He hoped that this was somehow still the case. And he hoped that I was taking advantage. I was so proud to have his letters, and especially the postmark from Israel, that I left them on my desk, so I could see them every day.

But I had yet to have a Jesuit professor head one of my philosophy courses, instead it was a rather unattractive and spiritless lineup that I was given to choose from. I had another round of the ancient Greeks with Dr. Mary Agonies O'Gallagher. The students really seemed to go in for her. And probably because of her unbridled digressions. She could make of any topic a segue into the problems of fat and fiber in our diets. I learned more by observing the behavior and comparing the mentality of Dr. O'Gulagger than I did about anything to do with ancient Greek philosophy. All of *that* stuff I was learning on my own.

And Father Dunn was a constant presence, making himself available to anyone who required divine intervention. I have this image of him with his team cap on backwards, and it'll make me smile, it'll make me smile and shudder. It makes me wonder how Tommy must have zoomed through Heaven, line drive home run to Cooperstown. Anyhow, the spring and summer times were always difficult for me. Difficult times to weather. *Come spring, comes a circus,* that's what Aunt Gloria says. The extra sunlight, and then the sudden and sometimes overwhelming warmth, and what with all the chemical and biological reactions going on, these play havoc with the sensibilities. I'm sort of involuntarily given over to the elements, I'm given over to nature, which is remarkable, I think, because if I'm a creature *of nature,* then why does my *given-overness* seem *involuntary?* I become unable to begin and last-out a project, I can only accomplish odds and ends sorts of things, like maybe a fragment of a thought or of a dream or of a poem or of a memory into my notebook, or maybe, if I'm not too restless, a correspondence. Nature is blind, and she has no heart. I suppose the time is easiest for the plants. Suddenly and gradually the conditions around them become suitable and they commence agerminating and to grow. *No questions asked.* Their only difficulties, it seems, are the immovable obstacle pebble, the stubborn tree root, the ravenous and merciless blue mole, and then the keen and hyperactive gardener, the rakes for smoothing broken ground, and dogs and cats and squirrels, of course, and of course Demeter's herbicide. Growing up, methinks we are so like the blades of grass, as we are *shaped* by the terrain we come up against. *And if there pushed any ragged thistle-stalk above its mates, the head was chopped, the bents were jealous else.* The birds sure seem to enjoy themselves. How they commence achirps and build for nestlings. Farmyards resound the extra lusty *doodle-doo.* They seem, I think, rather relieved, as at last they've something to do, *other than to forage for food.* It's not so easy for the animals, though. Their noses really get going. The thaws release to spell. *Whiff, whiff, whiff-a-her. Whiff, whiff, whiff-o'-him.* Dogs behave most pathetically at springtime, they're always looking to their masters with this distraction in their eyes, and especially the neutered ones. *Cut the sex out of 'em and all they've left to live for is food.* Then again, maybe we're doing them a favor. There's nothing so pathetic as a lost and trembling dog, *with the tail between the legs.* Let's see, I know Cashew, Bartók, Mimi, Lou, and who was it named her dachshund, Vivaldi? *These dogs live in my building.*

What I miss, I suppose, is bolting out of class into the springtime afternoon, and teaming up with my classmate and otherwise partner-in-crime, Bobby "the straightedge" Allison. We called him *straightedge* because the first time he shaved he borrowed his dad's straightedge razor and damn nearly cut the round of his chin off. Together we'd make a beeline for St. Vincent Ferrer High on 65th, where we'd hide and watch for the Catholic girls to sneak between the parked limousines and pull down their uniform skirts and pull up their jeans. The Ferrer girls had this *chic,* they'd be seen in their jeans and loafers while on top they still had on their school shirts and neckties. It was always the same two girls, *our cupcakes,* we called 'em. *Blonde with cream in the middle.* We would follow them home. They'd make believe they didn't see us, they'd make believe we weren't following and this we construed as just so much *icing.* They knew we were watching, and they knew we had our noses to the ground because they'd never head straight home. They'd lead us, rather, on some escapade, usually through the boutiques on Lexington and into Bloomingdale's where up at the Intimates they'd mess around with the bras and underpants and teddies and disappear into the dressing room together. And like, we knew they were taking their clothes off in there, *they knew we knew they were taking their clothes off in there.*

Michelle O'Garro was a Ferrer girl. We were becoming pretty close. We'd have our lunch together and meet for coffee between classes, we'd sit at the same table in the library, I would walk her to the subway station. I asked her over a couple of times, to see my books and my piano, but she said no, or else she'd say, not today. Then one sunny, warm afternoon we started walking along Central Park South and wound way the hell up outside my building. She came up and I introduced her to my books, and then I read one of my poems for her, and then I played Für Elise on my piano, and then we shared a beer.

It was weird. We fell asleep on my bed. I remember we were sitting on the bed, we were looking at my collection of Edward Gorey covers and talking about books and finishing off the beer, when the next thing I know I open my eyes and find her fast asleep with my pillow in her arms. It was already six-o'clock.

—That beer knocked me out, she said.

We washed our faces and went around the corner for some Chinese food. There's this take-out place on First called Ding Dong Wok. In their window they've this flashy neon-sign cartoon of a little sort-of-American-looking boy with freckles and a baseball cap. In his hands are a pint of noodles and a pair of chopsticks. He's supposed to be eating, lifting the noodles to his mouth, and the speech balloon sizzles in alternating, *My tongue Ding Wok. My tongue Dong Wok.* It's all rather *kitschy,* I suppose.

Michelle lived way the hell over in Brooklyn Heights. About eight-thirty she said she had to leave and at first I thought of walking her to the station but then I thought of calling the car service. She said no, but I insisted.

—You'll be home in twenty minutes, I told her.

I called down to the doorman, Mr. Nichols. Doormen know how to orchestrate these things, and it gives them something to do so at Christmas time they don't feel so guilty when you give them the envelope. I offered to pay the fare. She was a little embarrassed.

—My father will pay when I get home. . . .

And then she kissed me on my lips. I took her by the waist and held her close for a moment, and it turned into a hug. She had her head on my shoulder, and I could see her face and how her eyes were closed, and I just knew by how she was holding me, and how so natural and genuine it was.

We were together again on the weekend. We had no real plans except to walk around the Village and Soho and maybe see a movie or check out a jazz club. I'm not so crazy for jazz, I sort of feel for jazz the way I do for baseball. It's not by a long shot my first love but it gets ya into heaven so I sort of make allowances for it. I mean, I wouldn't complain about it, I can appreciate it and all, it just doesn't appeal to me. We were looking in all the windows of the art galleries in Soho. Most of what we saw was glaringly conspicuously agitprop and seemed like nothing at all to do with art *per se* but rather all about raising consciousness. In the Meat Epoch, making art is more about depicting and broadcasting some political struggle or dissent than it is about anything to do with *form* and *technique*. Everything's a rant. Everything's an editorial. And it's very *chichi* to be thought of as subversive, as an activist. The artists and the critics have, like, *transmogrified* it all into some or other *praxiology,* and everything is measured by its degree of political efficacy. Most of what we saw was bad, and not merely indifferently bad but bad so as to suggest some sort of perversion.

But then this one piece of conceptual art had us fixed. We were at this place on Wooster Street and they had this installation going on. These long banners like flags or pennants were hanging from the ceiling, and they all had these sorts of messages or captions scribbled in a sort of *graffiti* style on them. This one particular pennant began with the word *Libya,* and the word *Libya,* via this sort of series of *transmogrifications,* becomes the word *Labia.* . . .

—It's a statement on the way Muslim women are treated, braved Michelle. Like how they have to wear those *veils* to cover their lips. To the Muslims the woman's lips are. . . .

She broke off, searching for the polite expression.

—*Instruments of generation?* I offered.

Another of the pennants, *or whatever they were supposed to be called,* began with the word *antenna,* and midway through its series of transmogrifications became the word *return,* and then again, through another series of *transmogrifications,* became the word *sender.*

—Like this one here, she said, lifting her smile to the red and yellow pennant, reminds me of an Elvis Presley song.

—*Teddy Bear?*

—No. *Return to Sender.*

I so enjoyed the Michelle sensibility. She had her own distinctive talent for figuring an angle into things. She could go off on a roll on just about anything. And her sense of what seems real and true was honest and sound, her estimation of the worth of things was fair and not at all farfetched or highfalutin.

That evening, we were resting side by side upon my bed, our bellies were full and we had just finished a vodka. We were enjoying some moments of silence. We were facing each other and our eyes were open. We were smiling, and I thought we were communicating something. Then it all went weird on me. Her face began to remind me of a newborn kitten, so utterly vulnerable, and in need of caress. I wanted to caress her, then, and stroke her body, and make love to her, but I could not bring my hands to take her—and despite how lovely she was, and how apparently desirous she seemed. And then, little by little, I saw how her smile disappeared, and I realized what her gentle expression had been meaning to communicate.

—I know I'll never get to know you as well as I'd like to, she said. I know I'll never get to know you. That's all. I'm not saying I'm in love with you. Only you're not up to giving me the chance. . . .

Michelle has this old hat box full of hair bands and ribbons and barrettes she told me about. All real tortoise shell. Some of them she said were her grandmother's. She took the one off her head and showed me where it had a hairline fracture in it. She said she repaired it with some glue.

There was this exercise we used to do in gym class. You had to stand on one leg and stretch out your arms and stretch out your other leg high out behind you, like an airplane, while the instructors stand in front of you and *grade* your balance and co-ordination to see if you weren't perhaps somehow spastic or in some sense meningitic or something. They'd keep us standing there, in this *airplane posture,* like a troop of Hitler youth at a fitness rally. Bobby Allison—the same Bobby, who, history will show, was the first to keep the bay rum in his locker, and who, history will also show, said he got the idea from the black kids, he said the black athletes splashed it on after a workout.

Bobby Allison modified *the airplane* somewhat by bringing his right arm forward into a not altogether incongruous *Sieg Heil.* And we'd all start whispering in German to one another. Things like *jawohl* and *verboten* and *Geistesgeschichte.* There's this game we used to play in the schoolyard, some of the boys called it *bombardment* and some of the boys called it *nuke 'em,* but none of the boys ever called it dodge ball. You played it with one of those soft, red, almost-basketball-size playground balls that make that hollow sort of *ping,* almost a little *tinkle* sound, when you bounce 'em. Sometimes we used a volleyball, but volleyballs are too hard and rigid, you really need to get a firm grip on the thing, ya wanna be able to squeeze it. This game is a sort of adaptation of this other game they used to play outside the old Settlement Houses you used to find in old-ethnic-New York or otherwise underprivileged neighborhoods. Settlement House directors were usually these social welfare workers, or Catholic priests, or policemen volunteering their time, or idealistic public school teachers, even. I bet the meanest stickball games happened outside Settlement Houses. Anyway, to play this game, first you choosed up sides. It didn't matter how many players on a side, it depended on who wanted in. You could have five, ten, twenty—like I said it was a matter of who wanted in. And this game is best played on a basketball court—and always full court, never half court. Each team takes up positions on opposite sides of the midcourt line. First rule is you can't step across the midcourt line, you have to remain within your half of the court. To begin, two players meet at center circle, each facing his own team, his back to his opponents—because just as in basketball, they're gonna jump for the ball. Meanwhile the teams are positioning themselves, readying themselves to receive the ball. It's risky to stand at the restraining circle 'cos if you don't get the ball you're likely to be bombarded by the player who does. See, the object of *bombardment* is to hurl the ball at the opposing players, and to hurl it with such velocity, or, *french*—now *french,* now that's a fast spin so that it wobbles, sort of like a model strutting down a runway, you know how they walk one foot before the other so's to make their legs and behinds protuberate. Well you hurl it *so* that it'll hit the other player without him catching it, *and without its bouncing off his body and being caught by one of his teammates!* If you get hit by the ball, you're disqualified, and of course that means you're out of the game. But if you catch the ball—which is the whole damn point—the hurler is disqualified, *he's* out of the game. So this goes on, hurling the ball back and forth, until one team eliminates all the players on the other team. But there's a whole other dimension to the game, and it comes into play quite unexpectedly. At any moment during the course of the game, the ref is likely to call out *FOUL LINES!* This signals that a new rule has come into play. *Now you may cross the midcourt line and chase your opponent up to his foul line!* Of course this also means that you have only to behind your own foul line to retreat to. So at any moment, your opponent, *should he happen to have possession of the ball,* may be able to chase you back to behind your own foul line, *and just when you thought you were gaining some momentum!* So, as so many of our games are in a sense metaphors for life, *life, in a sense, is bombardment.* You're playing along, ducking on some shots, making some terrific catches, and getting in one or two good hits when all of a sudden Christ calls *FOUL LINES!* and it's like coming down with mono.

What do you think you two were communicating?
Desire, I suppose.
Did you love Michelle?
I don't know. I think she gave me mono.

Seriously?

I'm serious about everything.

Literally, then. As a matter of fact?

As a matter of fact I was miserable all summer. I kept on thinking about that dimwitted pennant-thing and how I saw Lydia between Libya and Labia, and of course I couldn't tell her that. And then how Schopenhauer says the beard is a sort of pubic hair. For Chrissake!

So then you did not love Michelle?

I don't know. I'm not exactly sure what I felt for her. I'm not exactly sure what I wanted from her. Friendship? I was lonely. I suddenly felt all desolate and isolated. All out of touch.

You were concentrating on your philosophy, and on your school work.

I was concentrating on my philosophy. My school work had become an unwelcome interruption.

You weren't sleeping well.

I was exhausted. I was too exhausted to convince her otherwise.

Convince her of what?

Of maybe giving me a chance. Of maybe working on me a little 'til I came around.

Came around to what?

To seeing that she was worth the effort. Maybe she realized that it was me, that I wasn't worth the effort. Probably that is what I communicated. Actually I think she read me pretty well. She's a smart girl.

So you communicated it to her the only way you were able to. That's okay.

That I wasn't worth the effort?

That you were not in a position to give her what she deserved. It's a compliment to you that this young lady thought enough of you to trust you as far as she did. And that you didn't go ahead and make love to her when your heart wasn't into it. She knows, Stephen, she knows what you did. And you in turn gave her a compliment.

I couldn't reciprocate on her feelings. The pheromones were jumping. And that can sometimes indicate an affinity. It was the first time in my life I had the opportunity to do it and I didn't take advantage of the situation.

And that's because you're a man, now. You're no longer a boy. A man has to act for real. It's no longer play time. Everything you do is representative of who you are and of what you value.

And she was lovely. She was lovely all over. I think I disappointed her. I know I did. We just came together, and then we parted. I just wanted to be alone from then on. I was sleepwalking into everything. Into people. Into relationships. Into these antagonisms with my professors at school.

Stephen, professors are like anybody else. Like anybody else they fall into ruts. You're challenging them on a deeply personal level, and some are going to react defensively.

Philosophy is not like the other subjects. It's not like mathematics or geography. A professor in philosophy is not necessarily a philosopher. My professors are not philosophers, they're more like historians. The philosopher has a special gift of interior verbal articulation, and most importantly he can discern the complementarities that exist in nature, and in the psychology of human nature.

All you can do is try to learn what these professors have to teach you. If the professor is not a genuine philosopher, you can't hold that against him. If they seem overly critical of you it's probably because they sense that with you they can raise the stakes a little higher. And you too have to rise to the challenge. You can't present a challenge and then once it's accepted fall back into your own comfortable disappointment. There are rules to the game. There are rules to be observed. The professor has the upper hand. That's rule number one! You have to accept that. You either prove yourself to be the genuine article or they'll begin to think you're a crank. Accept it, Stephen. Look, Stephen, think well of Michelle. Think sweet thoughts of her. She knows the truth and she will cherish the memory of you. I promise.

"The Remarkable Ms. Dorothea Russell"

But of all my new acquaintances one person stands out as most representative of who I was, and of how I got to be me. Or else I seem to have this habit, maybe it's a disposition, but rather like some karma magnet, of gravitating toward these real hard-edged people. Real psychological hard-liners. Afflicted sorts. Sometimes they all merge together into one horrific personage, or purgatory.

It was the fall semester of my second year, I was, I now contend, prolonging the agony, taking but twelve credits a semester, or three philosophy courses, my rationale being so as not to bog myself down in too much work. My two-year plan was racked out to three. I was enrolled in a course entitled *Truth in Kierkegaard and Wittgenstein.* Now I suppose that sounds highfalutin, but I assure you neither Kierkegaard nor Wittgenstein was of the highfalutin sort, they were, rather, down-to-earth and highly self-critical and solitary men. College professors love to think up these very highfalutin-sounding course titles, with words like *Truth, God, Death, Dilemmas, Text* and *Gender* in them. It was in fact a graduate seminar, led by one prof Dr. Charley O'Gallagher, wouldn't-you-know-it-spouse to Dr. Mary Agnes O'G. Prof Dr. C. O'G had one immediately outstanding characteristic, the distinctive smell of beer on his breath. It's not the same as when a prof revs up with coffee and a smoke before class, for in the case of prof C. O'G, he was mustering up some enthusiasm. Less outstanding, but no less odious, methinks, was his method of assembling and presenting the course material. Prof C. O'G would either clip out or photocopy sections of introductions and other sections of secondary source material and collect these rather disparate pieces together to form what was, ostensibly, his lecture notes, this in contrast to composing his own original lecture, or, *narrative,* and perhaps, however fortuitously, granting his class a fresh perspective. This *farce* was clearly in evidence, first because I ever followed along with the book he had lifted from—I kept it on my lap so's not to spook him, *while not once did he give mention to his source!*—and second because you could actually see that he had taped the photocopied and clipped *sections* into his portfolio—which was in fact but a hodge-podge mass of dog-eared and torn and rejoined pages. *But surely, if a student did this, would he not fail?* Another odious trait I discovered when, having occasion to enter his office, I spied inside his cabinet a whole row of library books, and some of the same that I'd been searching for myself ever since I'd learned of their usefulness. Profs can *borrow* from the library without worry for the sort of time restrictions that apply to students, so they can in effect monopolize or *hoard* a title—*whichever the case may be*—practically interminably. *What makes him feel so important that he should cut off access to these books? Are these the books that he has lifted from, perhaps?* Prof Dr. C. O'G was not particularly PC, but he was not in any sense *otherwise* either, and rather because he belonged to that, oh, docile and spineless *camp* and prudently-if-not-cautiously side-stepped and disclaimed with *but this is not my personal opinion* did he seem but an irresolute if not totally emasculated middle-classified *passive-blank* sperm bank. And no doubt it was this same lack of inspiration and enthusiasm, which had so *unabled* him to teach well and accrue for himself some intellectual authoritativeness, no doubt it was this same lack of passion that accounted for his need to swig down a beer before class. Prof Dr. C. O'G, as was the case with his spouse, was a distraction, a mediocrity in motion, *another obstacle to be endured, if not hurdled.*

With increasing certainty, and with ever increasing disillusionment, it was becoming clear to me how in college you must learn for yourself, how in college you must in effect teach yourself. Professors are a necessary matter-of-course which one must do his very best to oblige, that is pretend a disposition of conviviality towards, or else risk unpopularity. For professors talk to one another about their students, and word'll circulate that you're on to them, and they'll make of you an object of contempt. You see, professors think they're at the center of it all, that they are the heart and the students are the blood that flows. Well they're dead wrong. At the center of it all is the curriculum, and the curriculum has progressive heart disease.

There was another distraction present at that seminar, competing for my attention, only this one smelled better. Dorothea Russell was a successful model turned even more successful film producer. Her first projects were promotional presentations for garment industry sales seminars, these were really only slickly produced filmed fashion shows, and from there she did some long-running and what were considered breakthrough TV commercials, and then she produced some documentaries for public television. She did some music videos for this underground New York club band but unfortunately the band broke up after the lead singer died with AIDS and for some or other probably business reasons the videos were never released. There was an article about him in the *Times.* She showed it to me and said she had no idea he was unwell, and probably because his *shtick* was to pretend the appearance of a vampire. Dorothea wasn't Christian, in fact she was Jewish. Her given name was Dora Lifshitz. She said she had at one time considered herself a *secular* Jew, but even then the sense of ethnocentrism was appalling to her. So now she just considered herself *Dorothea Russell.* She none the less held this deep affection for Thomas Merton and Mother Teresa. And she knew all about Padre Pio and was big on the whole stigmata thing. She also enjoyed, and I could not help but notice, getting all sorts of chummy with the Jesuit professors. She would hug her books to her chest in the manner of a school girl and gaze up to them all starry-eyed, but as though her fondness had gotten the better of her.

Now Jesuits are not staid or in any sense old-ladylike, in fact they're usually impeccably neat and manicured, and some are downright athletic. I suppose I was a little jealous. Anyway, Dorothea had undergone some sort of crisis in her life that had resulted in a change of lifestyle. She was now a full-time scholar and mystic. She had collected all these sort of famous photographs of herself into this enormous mural-size collage that was affixed to her studio wall. It proved how beautiful she once was. It was plain that Dorothea had just burned herself out, so to speak. Sometimes it was apparent that she had partied a bit too hardily. You could see it in her face, she had these sort of smile lines. She was still unbelievably attractive, though, and what got me most was how she had genuinely come to feel insecure about her looks. Now she was just trying to figure it all out. When you go through life knowing people who wish only to sell your face and take you to bed, and not necessarily in that order, it must be refreshing to meet men who wish only to stimulate your mind. All that remained of Dorothea's former life were the books, the cat, the Greenwich Village brownstone, and a seventeen-year-old daughter named Dawn.

All I was told about Dawn, leading up to our being introduced, was that she had not long ago suffered an injury, a fall, during her dance lesson. She had been studying some sort of modern dance with some *name* somewhere uptown, and while attempting some particularly difficult movement had landed incorrectly and had crushed her ankle. She was off the crutches, now, but she still moved unevenly, and she was still on medication for the pain. According to Dorothea, the effect of her uneven step was to make her seem slightly tipsy, but that is until she spoke, or simply raised her face to counter your expression, what came across then was a categorical *keep your distance.* Her coolness aside, Dawn was a voluptuous beauty, a living doll, with waist-length rosewood hair, huge dark eyes, and God-given swollen lips. She did not have the tall, thin frame that her mother had, but all her own she was perfectly proportioned, and had a blessedly lean and athletic breast that rippled through her skin-tight leotard. When we arrived she was sitting at her easel, her hair was glistening in the sunlight. She was reading a book by Aldous Huxley, and in between she was drawing what looked to be a caterpillar. When Dorothea told her I was a poet, she turned to me and asked pointedly, *what else do you do?* I'm a student, I told her. *A philosophy student?* Dorothea broke in and said Stephen's my classmate. *My name is Zen Valium,* she replied, then turning back to her crayons. *Hello Zen Valium,* I said, to the back of her head.

Dorothea practiced reincarnation, but this was not of that literal back-to-the-flesh variety reincarnation, rather hers was a metaphorical rebirth. According to Dorothea, you can discharge your past—its restrictive or in her case decadent fetters—and begin your life anew, so long, of course, as the mortgage payments continued. She said it was a lot like finding God, only, it was the overcoming of her tendencies, and that she found was dependent upon the strength of her will and of her imagination.

—But what of the others in your life? I asked. What of family and friends and business people? Do they perceive and understand the change? Are they sympathetic? I think most persons rather cynical and suspicious, and inclined to ridicule, and if only because they reckon themselves practical, with their feet planted firmly in reality, planted firmly in the ethical, that is. They may well deem you an eccentric. Are not most persons scoffers and sneerers, envious and petty and resentful of anyone who should dare such, such a leap?

—Satisfy your commitments. *Render unto Caesar.* It is the overcoming of the automatic and spontaneous. The overcoming of the involuntary. A renewed sense of control and responsibility. And a renewed consideration for those upon whom your actions turn. It is an increased awareness, born of a renewed sense of self. *It is the birth of conscience.* You speak of *persons,* Stephen. I do not use that term. I speak of *individuals.* It is a rare find, I think, the *person.* Personality is not a given in life. One must *choose* to become a person. What we *are* born with, what *is* a given, is the tendency, *the unconscious tendency,* to acquire for ourselves traits and habits, patterns of behavior, and these from the sources at hand, the nearest and most dominant—our parents, our elder siblings, *our religion.* Examine your life, Stephen. Discover for yourself an identity. Become a *self. A personality.* Fate can guide you only so far, however conspicuous her congruity. Although I think you quite the exotic bird enough. Only then can you know true responsibility, for your self and for others. Only then can you know the true significance of your self and of others. Only then can authentic reliable participative being begin. The bourgeois status quo will endure, if only because it has nowhere to go.

Or,

so much depends
upon

a
Brooks Brothers suit

neatly
pressed

beside the white
broadcloth shirt

Then again, maybe it's all just a matter of getting up on the right side of the bed for a change. I was later to understand how Dorothea had suffered a terrible shock, a nervous breakdown sort of shock. This in fact was the catalyst to her exploration and discovery of her personality and selfhood. But she recovered on her own. She is her own heroine. And she was speaking from experience.

According to Dorothea there is but one great mystery most deserving of our reverence, and that is the mystery of love. Love, and its affects, she told, is the most popular occasion for our resorting to mysticism, whether in the form of the consulting of the Chinese *I Ching* oracle, the burning of scented candles, the reading of the tarot, or simply consulting the daily horoscopes.

I was inclined to take her at her word on this, but I was, however, somewhat familiar with the *I Ching* oracle. Lydia owned a copy and we sometimes asked it questions. I remember its once telling me, *but was it in response to a school matter?*

Slow going
on the George,
upper deck
still closed for repairs

And I knew well, of course, those bizarre, unsubtle candles, the rather gaudy colored wax inside those tall glass tubes. Sometimes the wax was green, and there were shamrocks and dollar signs on the glass. I know them well from shopping Woolworth's.

Dorothea had plenty to say regarding love. She'd never refer to her own history but I could tell it was knowledge gained by trial and error. She spoke about this sort of *hold* a woman sometimes gains upon a man. It has to do with *satisfaction.* The sort of satisfaction lovers give. *Sexual satisfaction,* to be specific.

—You might think a man gets hooked on a woman for the satisfaction she gives him, she told. Such is not an unlikely case. And their satisfaction may be mutual. However there exists another and just as common hold.

It was fast becoming clear how Dorothea had perhaps missed her true calling in life. She should have been a professor. *Mystery and Manners 101.* Lab fee negotiable. Or perhaps she would become a Sufi. For she so dearly wished to impart knowledge. The more we had of these rather impromptu discussions—at her home, at the café, before and after class—the more they took on the manner of a Platonic dialogue, with she quite naturally assuming the status of the mentor, and I the insipid interlocutor.

—It is not the satisfaction *she* gives *to him,* she continued, that so inflates his self-esteem, and so causes that self-esteem to be so passionately determined. On the contrary, it is the satisfaction he believes himself to be giving *to her,* and indeed bound up with her communication of this, that so inflates his self-esteem, such that he wants her, *needs her time and again.*

—Well I admit to being more concerned for how *she* is getting on than how I am, I said. So you're saying, it is not the satisfaction she gives to him, *that has him hooked,* but rather the satisfaction he believes himself to be giving to her.

—His self-esteem becomes bound up with what he perceives is his ability to sexually satisfy, *to overcome,* his woman. This is a form of domination.

—Well, yes. I suppose it is. And on a somewhat rudimentary level. Although it does seem rather sophisticated. But really, who is dominating who? It seems to me the woman is in this way manipulating the man.

—She is. And indeed many men reach a high degree of fulfillment this way.

—Which makes them all the more susceptible, I would imagine. But, in that they believe they are dominating their women? Or in that they believe they are sexual champions? Either way, seems to me the women are running the show. Are men in fact so easily deceived? If such is the case then what are the feminists complaining about? Seems to me, then, it's just a matter of having so well controlled us from the whore house, they now wish to control us from the White House. And we like it!

Dorothea has this angle on the psychology of women's dress, that how while some women dress for power, other women dress for sex. It's about what makes a woman feel alive. The feminists are wont to dress for power, which is why they'll often dress and seem of masculine mien, as a sense of power is what makes them feel alive, and as they construe so much to be the title of the male. But then the usual gal'll dress for sex, will dress so as to be attractive and sexy, and even a bit risqué, for to exude sexual attraction is what makes her feel alive, and what serves *her* sense of power. For *to feel powerful* is to feel alive. *To feel alive* is to feel a sense of power. *You pays your money and you takes your choice.*

"Que sçais je?"

Most primitive peoples have held the belief that labor was a voluntary act upon the part of the child, due to its desire to escape from its confinement in the womb. The midwife who assisted at the birth did all she could to coax out the child by promises of food, and resorted to threats if the child was obdurate. The expectant mother was even starved during the last week of her pregnancy in order that the child might be more willing to emerge and obtain the milk that awaited it.

The character of the labor undergone by the mother was referred to the disposition of the child, all difficulties were blamed upon its evil disposition. This belief afforded good grounds for the destruction of the child by efforts at forcing its delivery and even by instruments designed for this purpose, since a child so perverse as to refuse to be born merited death, as did the mother who carried such a child.

If the labor of the child-bearing woman was difficult, assistance of the straight forward sort might be called into play. She was picked up by the feet and shaken, head down, or rolled and bounced on a blanket, or bound to a stake on the open plain in order that a horseman might ride at her with the apparent intention of treading on her, only to veer aside at the last moment, and by the fear thus inspired aid in the expulsion of the child. She might be laid on her back to have her abdomen trod upon, or else be hung to a tree by a strap passed under her arms, while those assisting her bore down on a strap over her abdomen.

It was a privilege to be let in on Dorothea's insights. And these were cautionary insights, to boot. I saw how true it could be, and of its greater implications—I saw how utterly true and pathetic it was and it made me cringe with embarrassment.

—Have you ever listened to a couple argue? she asked. The way they curse each other and the oaths they make? The real and explosive hatred and disappointment and disbelief they express?

And I was thinking of Lydia's mother, she once struck her husband in the ankle with a driver, seems they were arguing over the wood grain in the dining table, she was insisting it looked like a salmon steak. Lydia was present when it happened and it frightened her and threw her into hysterics. She started ripping at herself and pulling at her hair and really injuring herself. She was trying to draw her mother's attention away from her father, who was decidedly down for the count. That's the last she remembered after she woke up in the hospital, in a room across from her father, who was sent home that same evening. The driver had perfectly contacted the solid rubber heel of his shoe and had merely stunned the man. But for Lydia it was a different story. She had really injured herself. They kept her in for several days, under sedation, and under the proverbial *observation*. That's how she began her psychoanalysis. And she had always warned me about ever freaking out and doing hysterical things in her presence.

—I think that's one of the reasons how I lost her, I said. I began to disregard how sensitive she was. I was taking her for granted. She warned me she was frightened by deranged acting-out.

Dorothea sighed, shaking her head for the logic of my lesson.

—Well I'd been seeing a doctor all my life, I said. And I suppose I trusted that with Lydia, I could get away with anything.

—There's something you have to understand, she began. Sometimes it's not about you. Sometimes it's about the other person. Sometimes it's not your episode and you are only bearing witness.

She took my hands and brought my arms around her body, and that's how our first embrace happened. I felt so raw and awkward. I was praying for her to take control of me, and to make love to me. And she said, *I'm giving you my love, Stephen.* And she took control of me, and she made love to me.

Dorothea was an aristocrat, albeit in a self-styled sort of way, if such a thing is possible, but time and again she was perfectly on, perfectly in control, of her voice and of her mien, and of her conduct and rapport. It did seem I was her only friend, or else so far as *this* station of her life was concerned for while she seemed to have countless acquaintances and business associates—and this was clear from the number of messages and the many cards and letters—I never once knew her to return a call, or to return a correspondence, or to receive a guest. She had accepted me to be her confidant, her companion in study. I was the only person, so far as I could tell, to be welcomed into her home, and to be made to feel at home there. And this *proscription,* again so far as I could tell, included Dawn's acquaintances. I never knew her to have a friend up to her room or to go out to meet with anyone, or to speak of anyone other than herself or of her mother. With Dawn I couldn't help but to be shy and reluctant, I was cautious of asking questions, of making overtures lest I turn her away and alienate her, and possibly sour our situation. And I knew this was obvious to Dorothea, and I wondered if it was obvious to Dawn and if it was indeed obvious, well, when, then, would she relax her guard and allow us to be friendly?

I was spending all my weekends there, at the brownstone in the Village. I was sleeping in the guest room, which was on the studio floor, one floor above their bedrooms. In addition to a library, the studio had its own small kitchen, so in the mornings I could make my own coffee and have some time for myself before I dressed and before Dorothea came up to join me and begin our studies. Dorothea and I were being affectionate, but we were not, as a matter of course, lovers. For certain, I was too reluctant to initiate anything, and I knew she realized this, and I accepted how she was content with me for this, for it meant I would not create any awkward situations. But she also knew I was desirous. And I sensed how she was enjoying my distraction. As though to reward me for my good behavior, I was promised a treat for Christmas week, we were spending the week at her country house, in Sneden's Landing.

Gregory Vincent St. Thomasino

"Stephen's Landing"

The Italian sports car, its brake engaged, slid some inches on the driveway gravel before halting in its place beneath the portecochere. Reaching to the cupboard's upmost shelf, the girl withdrew glass tumblers. Clouds were gathering, wisps of glistening cirrus halted high above like monitors, sensing no resistance, they summoned their brothers, the cumulus, they arrived, arrived, increasing their number, then seemingly cumbersome they hovered, waiting, pondered a bumbling.

I have guttersnipe teeth. That's what Aunt Gloria says. I think it's motherly of her. Like, as though she found me in the gutter. My teeth are extremely sharp. Are they not somewhat caniniform? Observe, this is my demon face.

There's nothing wrong with your teeth. Don't grimace.

Eyetooth, bicuspid, incisor. My wisdom teeth came in impacted. I'm terrified of the dentist. Did I tell you that? The smell of clove and of antiseptic. I'm terrified of the drill. Just the sound of it. Or else you'd think they wanted you to lie there terrified and helpless. The smell of a drilled-into tooth can overcome me. It's the burning dentin. It's burning bone! The enamel is the hardest substance in the body. Bosch told me that. Bosch is something of a dentist. I have this scab on my shinbone. I don't know how I got it. And last night I was picking it, and I felt like a little boy again. It was a remarkable moment. The thing about babies is I just can't cuddle a baby the way I can a puppy or a kitten. Babies are just too fragile. And mothers say they're edible. Do you boil your chickens? Do you know why the sunlight falls in shafts? It's because the clouds are miners. That's how they get their silver lining. It's how you say your T's, Dr. P. It's a dead giveaway.

What does it give away?

You spit your T's. It says Upper West Side. Do you boil your chickens? My Auntie roasts her chickens. A little cranberry pudding on the side. It adds color to the plate. It's nothing, really, just a matter of woofer T versus tweeter T. It's nothing, really, just keep that T at the back of your mouth, is all.

You're annoyed with me for something. Do you want me to come around and sit beside you? Remember how we used to sit together? Equal partners?

That's how you made me fall in love with you. It was one of your tricks. And I tried to bite you. I wanted to eat you. I still do. I want to eat into the inside of your thigh. It's interesting, when it comes to roasted chicken I go straight for the wings and the drumstick, but when it comes to turkey, I'm strictly a breast man. Or else it's always the involuntary things. Smiling. Sobbing. Breathing. Orgasm is involuntary.

Do you remember these? Do you remember when you made these for me?

Of course I do. You wanted to see samples of my handwriting. And I did these, these in the morning. And I did these that afternoon. And I did these with you the next day. You said they looked like three different signatures, like three different persons wrote them. But then you told me it was just my body, it was my body's sensitivity to food. That's when I stopped drinking Pepsi.

"Stephen's Landing"

Taking up her file, the woman turned for another room. She placed a tape of de Hartmann into play and reclining began fashioning her fingernails—expertly, as but a life of habit could achieve. Now the music played, a hesitant, evolving resolution fit to entrance and deliver, delight the body into serial movements. She heard his footsteps, the creaking of the floorboards above.

—Stephen?

He loved her this way, as she gestures with her file, or, more concertedly, with her eyes.

He let a fingertip to beneath her eye and gently palmed her nape, and as he held her forward she parted her thighs and held him to her breast.

She saw, beyond his boyish countenance, an inner strength which had yet to be exerted. She saw other men, but only bodies, no voices, no personalities. She saw her ailing mother, and father long adieu. She saw her child—that gorgeous face, flaming hair given to the wind.

He held his head upon her breast, the ribbon cool to his warm face. He kissed above her heart, the scent of her perfume. He brought his palm to just beneath her breast. He kissed her chin. He kissed beside her mouth. She kissed his forehead. She touched her lips to his mouth and pressed his head to her breast.

—And I know *you,* Stephen, she whispered. *I've known you all my life.*

The fireplace was made of stone, stones the size of skulls, small skulls, set in cement. Smooth. Round. The blues and grays of buried slate. And there were flutes of branch, or tibia, buried into the cement. And I thought of our little bungalow, and of our black cast-iron belly stove, and for the first time in my life, I wished they had held onto it.

—Do the stones get hot? I asked.

No one answered.

Thea was tending to the fire. The logs were white and black and smeared with amber sap. And they were moldy and sweet smelling. She wore a pair of suede mittens. And when she went down on her hands and knees I saw, beneath her pleated kilt, I saw a little of her cheek. And I saw Dawn, then, and she was watching me.

—It's our only source of heat, Thea said, piling the logs and then lighting the kindling, and then placing it just so.

—Is there something I can do? I asked.

—We have loads of blankets, she said. *Dawn?* Stephen, take one for your lap. In a couple of hours we'll be roasting.

Dawn was mumbling to herself. She reached inside an old, battered trunk. I could smell the cedar on the wool. She sat herself on the sofa and covered her lap. She started rubbing her hands together, to make warmth. As she rubbed her rings were making clicking sounds. She knew it was annoying her mother, who was still on her hands and knees. Then she said, *if you stand next to the window you can see your breath. You can make frost on the window. We don't come here too often in the winter any more. Just to flush the toilets.*

—Thank you, Dawn, the mother said. Believe me, Stephen, it gets like a sweat house in here.

The girl was still all bundled up.

—I can tolerate just so much discomfort, she said.

And I thought she said the *so* rather deliciously, if somewhat like a college girl.

—May I see your rings? I asked.

I thought at least this would stop the clicking noise.

—*Dawn?* the mother said. Get some glasses down. *And the pear brandy.*

I was beginning to get the impression that we were there, for the most part—that is, aside from flushing the toilets—that we were there for my sake alone. When she returned I offered her my mittens.

—I've been keeping them warm for you.

She left the snifters and the brandy on the coffee table. And then she pulled the mittens off my hands. But as she did this, she made a face as though to say, *I still think you should keep your distance.*

I poured the brandy. I took mine and took a little taste, and then I put it down in one shot.

—Sometimes the pipes get frozen, she said. *And you have to make into a meat-loaf pan. And then you have to take it outside and dump it.*

—Winning, Dawn! the mother said, still on her hands and knees.

And it was difficult to keep my eyes from beneath her kilt.

The girl took a little sniff and then a sip of her brandy. She licked her lips, and then she put it down in one shot.

—*Mom! What are you doing to that fire!*

Dawn, just like her mother, had this habit of expressing herself downright bluntly, but audaciously. In the beginning I could not help but be nonplused but then I came to understand it was their own peculiar way of doling out a compliment. Indeed they were never boorishly rude, but only intentionally so. And yet to strangers and to neighbors, and to the uninitiate generally, they could play the utmost courteous and kind.

The brandy was kicking in. I started giving the girl the ole bird dog treatment, that's when you follow someone around with your eyes even though, *or despite that,* it's probably annoying them. I think she was enjoying it, however. I think she was beginning to accept me.

She went over to these two adjoining doors and, hesitating a moment, peeked in through the jalousie slats. She glanced at me over her shoulder, no doubt to see if I was still the bird dog—and I was, *I was getting a load of her hair*—then she pushed the doors apart. It was a closet, there was an old upright piano in there. She rolled it out somewhat and made a cushion with her blanket on the bench, then she removed the mittens and put them away inside her pockets. She started tapping out a scale. The strings were not exactly in tune. At first she hung around the middle C, then she spread it out some and became a little imaginative. Were it not for the rusty tuning, and for her rusty hands, I suppose she knew what she was doing.

I said, *I have a baby grand.* But she ignored me.

I started staring at the fire. It was blazing, now, and the place was indeed beginning to warm up. And I was getting a load of her hair, how shiny and smooth and *polished* it seemed. She began going in and out of fragments of a popular tune, but as though she had her doubts about playing it through. Then she burst right into it, it was The Beatles' Martha My Dear. It was a pretty bouncy rendition, too. She was about three quarters through when her mother came beside her and said play some de Hartmann for Stephen.

—Do you know the work of Thomas de Hartmann? she asked.

I shook my head, no.

—Dawn knows de Hartmann by ear.

She gently pushed her daughter's hair out of her face and then giving her a hug whispered something in her ear. I think she said, *I'm cooking now.*

I moved closer to the fireplace. I sat down on the rug, real close to it. I could almost touch the flames with my fingertips. Thea went back to the trunk and brought out two more blankets. She left one beside her daughter on the bench. The other she put around my shoulders.

—I like it here, I told her. I can feel it warming up.

I was enjoying the crackle and the smoke of the wood. And it was pleasing, the cedar must. Everything around us was old and worn and had this comfortable, lived-in feeling.

—I'll make some tea, she said.

She lit a pair of lamps and left into the kitchen.

—So who is this Thomas de Hartmann? I like it, I said.

—It's restful, Thea answered from the kitchen.

Dawn stopped playing. . . .

—They're like tone poems, she said, pressing her hands together at her lap.

Then she began anew, now on a different and just as exotic-sounding melody.

—It's considered sacred music, Thea said. He was Russian. He died in 1956. We have tapes of the works he composed with Gurdjieff. This one she's playing now is my favorite. It's called Kurdish Shepherd's Dance.

She returned to check the fire. *Are you hungry?* I shook my head, *yes.*

The de Hartmann played continuously. Thea loaded the player and the two tapes played in a loop. Now and then Dawn sat at the keys and played along. I then sat beside her and followed her hands. Each time I turned my eyes from her hands she turned hers too and for the moment we were eye to eye.

—I can pick it up, I said. Let me play the left hand.

The Kurdish Dance piece came on.

—I can play it, I said.

—Wait, she said.

She turned off the player. When she returned she took hold of my right hand and we began to play the piece together. Again and again, in a loop we played. We played 'til it was perfect. She never once relaxed her grip upon my hand. And at the end, Thea applauded.

Well for some time after that I contracted these dreams I've been babbling about, and the common denominator, the center of gravity in each is this image of aged meat—ruddy-black rather pungent-looking aged beefsteaks on hooks and my impression is of open sores. I reach to touch it—I don't know why I reach to touch it 'cause I'm, like, thoroughly repulsed—and it's now the paw pads of some cat, but of a great cat, like a lioness, and it occurs to me, this is Dorothea's vulva!

I'm at this band shell, it's the big, blue Guggenheim behind Lincoln Center and I'm sitting on a bench among strangers—busloads of elderly men and women and some have their noses in these gaudy-red oversized laminated menus. I know the menus are söuvenïrs. And these are tourists. And I say aloud, to no one in particular, Thank you! The women have these cheap black wigs on their heads—they're just, like, perching on their heads. I think a wind'll come along and they'll take flight. I'm thinking, good, then I'll just wait. I cross my legs and fold my hands at my lap, and then I unfold my hands and I realize they're all knobby and arthritic-looking. And then the bench becomes a church pew, but I'm still at the place with the band shell. I notice the men are wearing wide rep-striped neckties, but the colors are unfamiliar to me—they're not colors at all, but, just blacks and grays—and they're knotted all haphazardly, as though knotted by arthritic hands. I notice this one man, he's just a few rows ahead, he seems somehow familiar but I can't place his face, we seem to have this staring competition going on. I think it's hostile. And I'm thinking, how'd this shit get started? I'm trying to turn away, as though to turn away will defuse the situation, but I can't turn my eyes, and he's staring me down so intensely, so hypnotically, and as though he were about to swear at me, or else to get up and come over and pounce on me, and our eyes are locked, and he's really glaring. And so I shrug and shake my head to egg him on, to get it done, to get it over with, but he just turns, he turns away and looks back toward the band shell. And now there's music going on. But the shell is empty.

This Oriental man, from out of nowhere, taps my shoulder saying woman must have child or she very unhappy. Not mine, I'm thinking. And I'm thinking, this guy's bowlegged. He looks at me as though he just read my mind and goes stampeding off, in a huff, climbing the steps onto the band shell but before he disappears he turns his face, to me, and sways this, like, retarded ballet step while up out of his stomach he heaves this colossal clam onto the immaculate blue wall of the band shell. And I hear myself, in a little singsong, saying, that's a little foetus!

And now I see behind and above the band shell there's this giant billboard with these two naked blondes spraying each other with, I don't know, ginger ale? And the legend reads,

what women in the know know about women

I hear this charming voice asking, something else? And I know it, it's the Polish cupcake from the deli. Her old man had a shiny bald head and wore gold octagonal wire-rims. He used to bird dog all the boys. I'm in that deli, I can smell the pickles and the mustard and the franks and the sauerkraut. I have a ticket in my hand, I order Black Forest ham on pumpernickel. And Bobby, stroking his chin, says, cut by virgin hands. And this sweet smoke like exotic incense or old wood starts burning my eyes. This woman's voice creeps up from behind, saying,

It's better to be HYPER-sensitive than HYPO-sensitive!

I turn around, and it's Skye Bosch! And then a few days go by and I meet her for real. You see I saw her in my dream. I had a premonition! Also at this time I acquired this dreadful lump in my throat. I was forever gulping. I was really getting in touch with myself.

"This Merciless Gravity"

Every time Dorothea didn't like what her face was changing into she'd lower her eyes and swear under her breath, *this merciless gravity.* It wasn't just her face. Because business obligations had caught up with her she chose to sit out the spring semester. Right before my eyes she shifted gear from mystic mode to maven mode. She was again producing promotional films, this time for cosmetics products. She was working out of her brownstone, orchestrating affairs via phone and via email and text. I was showing up pretty regularly, habitually, I suppose, after class sometimes and sometimes on the weekend, just to hang out and make a pest of myself, or such was the impression I got. I wasn't participating in any of her activities, although she did have me out to the bank a couple times, and to the post office if it was early enough, and to the cleaners, even, and if only, I suppose, to get rid of me for a while. I wasn't taking to her maven mode. And she had put her studies on hold, which meant, I soon realized, that I was on hold too.

I let a whole two weeks go by without calling or showing up, just figuring she'd call to learn why not and then I'd say, like, *oh, I suppose I've been too busy,* but no, she didn't call. And then one afternoon after class I went over and she told me, *through the intercom,* to come back later. I suppose I was a little hurt by this, and I suppose I should have just gone home, but instead I hung around the Village for a while, and when I did go back, well, that's when I *contracted* Skye Bosch.

I was downstairs standing at the door, sort of meditating on which finger to use on the intercom button, when this messenger person shows up behind me with a pouch full of videos.

—You're here for Russell? I asked.

—Yes. *Did you press?*

It was late in the day, and it was getting pretty cold, the sun was pretty low by now. She seemed to be shivering. And I could not help but wonder if the ring in her nostril was causing her discomfort.

—Just about to, I said. Are you walking? It's pretty cold to be lugging things around.

—My bicycle was stolen.

—Really? Oh, too bad.

—Yes it is. *Did you press?*

Dorothea shouted down, *who is it!* I answered, *it's me— and I'm not alone there's a messenger with me!*

I was surprised and even challenged by how this messenger person, how having once gotten herself inside and having dropped off her pouch, began, *but with all convenience, then,* began to make herself at home. She removed her black leather *little wild one* motorcycle jacket, and then a black, *of course,* bulky turtle-neck, and then a long, black, *of course,* scarf that she had wound around her neck and chest, and then a brief but vital mirror stop and asked if anybody wanted tea.

Dorothea ignored her. I responded, and despite that she hadn't addressed me directly, *yes, please, I'll have some tea.* All the same she seemed to have ignored me. She fixed the kettle on the stove. She was familiar with the cupboard and where everything was kept. When she returned she sat across from me and pulled off her black *ass-kickin'* engineer's boots. She again with all convenience simply left the boots and folded up her legs beneath herself. I wondered, then, if she had indeed put on enough water. I had to get up to check the kettle. When I returned Dorothea said *Stephen, Skye Bosch. Skye, Stephen Child.*

—Stephen Child, I said, putting out my hand.

—Skye Bosch, she said, forcing a smile and giving my hand a little tug.

I thought, *Skye Bosch. Go figure.*

—That's a pretty name, I said in my best Alex de Large.

I think she was trying to avoid me. She replied by raising a corner of her mouth and her eyebrow simultaneously, as though she were in pain, and then her shoulder did this sort of twitch—not quite a true gesticulation, but rather totally involuntarily. She turned her eyes to the kettle, and then, lifting on the armrests, and with a little hop, she readjusted her legs.

—Well it's an *adorable* name, I said in my best John Houseman, making friendly with myself.

But I was really onto this nose-ring business, and then her clothes. *Rather brute,* I was thinking. She had a black, *of course,* thermal top on and the sleeves were too long so the wristbands were pushed up on her forearms, but then she pulled them down over her hands, like mittens, *or paw pads,* and bunched the wristbands up inside her fists. She had this long and heavy-looking inverted silver cross on a black leather thong around her neck, which didn't seem so much *Christian* as a little S&M. The knees of her jeans were slashed and frayed, and at her crotch—*I really must stop staring at her crotch.* But then her hair was a sort of giveaway. Anything but brute. Black dense curls, but snug like Sherpa wool, and covering her forehead in bangs.

—*That's teddy bear hair!* I said.

And that got Dorothea's attention. She turned from her work and made this remarkably ugly face. Meanwhile Skye had burst into a genuine and much surprising laughter.

—So, I started up, your bicycle was stolen. Did they leave you stranded?

—It was stolen from my apartment.

—No!

—*Yes!* They took my clothes. They took my cameras. All my CDs. They ate my food. They took my telephone. All my earrings. My watch. My socks. My bras. My underpants. Do you believe it? All my cash.

—That's quite a list.

—*They made in my toilet.*

—Did you disinfect?

—Fucked up my whole life.

I know that I was staring, and I knew that at any moment it could turn her off, but I couldn't help staring at her eyes. At how blue they were. They were reminding me of the blue in a painting by Matisse. *Bosch has eyes the blue surrounding Icarus from Jazz.*

—You have beautiful eyes, Bosch.

I just naturally took to calling her that.

—You do too.

We had our tea. And Dorothea told us to leave. We got dressed and we left. It was dark, now, and a whole lot colder than before.

—You know what, Bosch, I started. *Today's my birthday.*

I know it's sort of rude, telling someone you hardly know that it's your birthday. I mean, what are they supposed to say?

—Oh! *Happy birthday!*

I didn't feel so rude over telling it to Bosch, though. There was something in her way that told against any such decorum. *Like probably it was her clothes?* Anyhow I just needed to tell someone, so I figured it was her.

—Are you going out? she asked.

—No. I'm just going home.

And really, I couldn't handle another birthday at Aunt Gloria's. And if I phone her I know she'll bake a cake. If I phone her I'll have to go over there. And really, the whole Lydia thing. Just the thought of it made me cringe. And as for what Dorothea might be thinking, *well I knew she wasn't thinking about me.* What I really had in mind was how to get Bosch up to my apartment. And I was thinking, *if we become friends, then I could lend her some of my clothes.* I was, like, imagining her into my shirts, and into my briefs, even. And I was generating all sorts of affection for her, for this person I really hardly knew. And it was cold, and we both were beginning to shiver. The wind was tearing fast. Papers and grit and debris of all sorts was being swept around in whirlwinds through our legs. And I think I saw her nose ring *flap,* and I had to suppress my cringe. And I kept on catching this whiff of patchouli.

—I smell patchouli, I said.

—That would be me, she said, and then her shoulder did a twitch. I'm heading for the D train, to The Bronx, she said.

—I'll walk you to the station. . . .

I was thinking how my *No* to her question, about going out for my birthday, might have come off as uncouth, or maybe just too sincere. In the war between man and woman sincerity is not always a virtue. And it reminded me of something Professor Torrez's wife once said. *To be one-hundred percent honest in love is infantile.* And anyhow most people think you're a retard if you don't go out to party for your birthday. But birthdays were never a big deal for me, or else, the less said about them, the better.

Anyhow by this time my mouth had gone all sticky and dry, and I felt a little panicky, and I felt the return of the lump in my throat, which in itself gave me cause for worry, and I so much wanted to have her home with me. It's as though everything hinged on her reply, and the prospect of her *No* would mean thumbs down on my sainthood, for Chrissake. I felt I was going hysterical, any moment I'd be totally hysterical, any moment I could drop to the ground in a catatonic heap. I started gulping, trying to swallow my lump. I felt there was an invisible hand around my throat trying to choke me. *I'm really afflicted,* I was thinking. *I really do have a crisis, here.*

—Where do you live? she asked.

—East 56th. . . .

I couldn't speak more than two words at a time. And I had trouble saying the *sixth,* it sounded like a lisp. And it was awfully cold. The wind was tearing at our faces. I wasn't thinking when I took her arm, and with a tug started us walking, and she allowed me to 'cause when I took it she brought me close against her side. *And how this simple and perhaps meaningless gesture, roused my spirits, and gave me confidence!*

—Listen, Bosch, I started. I got a wok. Let's get some vegetables. We'll get some rice and whatever and we'll fix ourselves some dinner. *We can talk about Dorothea.*

—You mean at your place?

—Yes. At my place. Come on. Let's get a cab.

I think she was thinking it over. I was watching her shoulder and it looked like it was twitching. I was standing pretty close and the patchouli was a little overwhelming, but I told myself, *I can tolerate this. Maybe I can finagle her into my shower.*

—I'll need to get some cigarettes, she said.

—There's a grocer's on my corner. They have everything. Come on. *Let's get a cab!*

But when at last we reached my building we found Dawn waiting in the lobby. She rose when she saw us and seemed surprised as hell to see me with Skye Bosch. I don't think these two were very fond of each other. They didn't so much as say hello as downright sneer in each other's direction. And Dawn looked like she'd been crying, and I was picking up on this sense of urgency. Her eyes were red and swollen, her face was pale and unwashed, her hair was a mess. There was a suitcase on the floor behind her. . . .

—Can I come up?

Bosch was quick to seem reluctant and uneasy. I had to tell her twice to remove her stuff. Dawn asked where and went straight for the mirror. I gave Bosch a look and a shrug. She sort of curled her lip at me.

—Come on, then, let's start dinner, I said and waved for her to join me in the kitchen. I was emptying the groceries when I heard the door pull open and slam shut. I watched for her from my window. I saw her step out onto the sidewalk, pause a moment, then start away. Then Dawn reappeared.

—Hungry? I asked.

—Where's Skye?

—She left. *She just came up to borrow a book.*

—A book?

She was held up just outside the kitchen. She was giving the once-over to my books.

—Shaw's *Candida,* I said.

—She sure is peculiar. *And how about that radical pa-tchouli?* So, *Third World.* So, *au courant.* Sure leaves a trail. You know she sprays it on everything she delivers? My mother says it's her way of *being there,* even when she's not.

—Come 'ere. Put this stuff away.

—Whose are these? You smoke French?

She was holding Bosch's cigarettes. And now she was opening them.

—They *were* Skye's. Well now they're yours.

—Why are *her* cigarettes in *your* grocery bag?

—You'll have to ask the grocer. That's the way he packed 'em. I forgot to take them out for her.

She lit one up. And then she blew the smoke, straight up. Just like her mother does.

—You know, she's gonna want one, she said. *And then she's gonna throw a fit.*

—You know, would you like a drink? I think the situation calls for a drink.

The situation naturally gave me the upper hand, and I knew I had to take total advantage. It was the psychological edge I had needed over her all along. I took the vodka bottle out of the freezer and I reached for some glasses. Meanwhile she had gone back to her suitcase, and was returning with a bottle of pear brandy.

—Oh! Very nice! I said. *So later for this vodka.*

—I brought along some essentials, just in case.

I put the glasses back and instead got down my snifters. I couldn't help feeling bad for Bosch. And, curiously enough, it was in a happy sort of way, like what with how she so suddenly felt or, indeed, knew to have to leave that way, and how she left without taking her cigarettes. But then Dawn, and I suppose this is what made me happy, Dawn, and despite or perhaps because of her rather wild-looking and susceptible appearance, was beginning to seem desirable.

—We'll eat later, I said.

—Later? So I'm staying?

I took a little sip. She took a little sip, then licked her lips, then put it down in one shot. I naturally followed suit.

—Listen, I said, why don't you let me take a quick shower, and then we'll do something serious about dinner. Maybe we'll order some Chinese.

I filled my glass and left her to explore the place on her own. I always wanted to drink in the shower. I'm not sure why, exactly. Maybe it's the light. Or maybe it's because it's just plain boring. The water was just getting right when the room went dark and Dawn's naked leg stepped through the curtain.

—I don't think I can shower with you, Dawn. I just don't think I can just be naked with you here.

—I don't think I can shower with you, Dawn. I just don't think I can just be naked with you here.

She took the sponge and started soaping it up. I had to close my eyes. I was immediately aroused and I couldn't bear to witness what was happening. She started singing the happy birthday song.

And so I came to know the pleasures of bathing in the dark.

Fiat lux not!

The next morning she returned downtown, but so to fetch more clothes and all her toiletries. She was moving in. And I felt no compunction to prevent her.

Here is Dawn's breakfast plan. It consists of one room-temperature 20oz can of pineapple chunks, which she never finishes, a B-complex vitamin, a calcium-magnesium tablet, and half a 5mg tablet of diazepam, *but just to round off the edges.*

But of all the esoteric ideas Dorothea had seen fit to share with me the one that struck most keenly was perhaps the least esoteric of them all.

Honestly assess yourself.

Well, of course. But from what perspective? *Honesty?* The process is ultimately defamiliarizing. That's the effect it has. And then there's the *onion* idea, that says the person is like an onion in that the person is in reality composed of layer upon layer, or skin upon skin, each *skin* being some particular residue of experience, *or lifetime,* or else some sort of delusion or deception or fantasy or wish or shock or lamentation, or migraine, even, and at the center of it all, at the core, the deep within, at the quintessence, after you've chucked every stinking goddam layer, or skin, or residue, is, is what?

Utopia!

Is utter oblivion.
Afflictions may ultimately prove blessings.
Honest, Dr. Panic-of-Loss?

Along with the deconstruction of Man—
i.e., meaning
—following upon the heels of the deconstruction of God—
i.e., Meaning
—occurs the demagnetization of our compass.

Which is my very definition of Utopia.
The compass does not apply.

My consciousness is as a compass. But ever spinning, spinning with vehemence! My consciousness is as a lexicon, but I, perforce, repudiate grammar.
Honestly assess yourself.

I am under surveillance.

Stiletto heels.
Engine Co. No. 44 lipstick.
And then there is my face as it appears in the lower
left-hand edge of my dresser mirror.
It's rather pale, I think,
and on account of my angular cheekbones
and on account of my high forehead, my thin jaw line
and my twin chin,
am I not Cubist-looking?
Okay, then, I am Cubistman, the two-dimensional super hero.
I turn the villains into Cubist paintings. My lair,
a cigarette butt-strewn garret on the boulevard Voltaire,
is in fact a gallery of portraits.
And some of them are quite dramatic.

Rejection is obese, my darling *Dr. P.* And this residual
magnetic flux trapped inside my cranial sarcophagus is as a
dross distorting my view of an idyll.
Open your mouth!
But why?
Do it quickly!

Ahhhhh. Ach, du!

Just as I thought. We must remove those metal fillings at once. You're picking up somebody else's brain waves! But first, tell me, Stephen, do you hate these people?

Yes. And everyday. And for something new!

Or else,

The air is always sour outside *P.'s*. This corner, I am told, been told by darling *P.* herself, is one of our city's environmental hot-spots. And if you hang around here long enough, which is not too long at all, and I should know because I've done it enough, you'll gather soot inside your nostrils, and in your eyebrows, and on your forehead—

Then make a smudge. Play first day of Lent!

—and in your hair, and on your sleeves, and on your shoes and inside your pant cuff. And after rainfall—*but you must have noticed, I mean, after all, you office here*—the puddles are black. So no, please, I am not in distress. And no, please, we're not squirming today. But are you aware, there is a coat of soot on your desk?

Do these windows open?

Shall I let in some fresh air?

Honestly, Dr. P. Are you getting all this down?

Achoo?

"The Utter Verticality of the Plumb Bob"

So I suppose Dawn turned out to be pretty generous. Even with her drugs, although the painkillers made me nauseous. But the diazepam was ever so agreeable, it never failed to ward off my lump, or, really this *fist* that was clamping at my throat. And *Dr. P.* was quick to make out my prescription. *One hundred and twenty, one 4 times a day.* But this *one 4 times a day* business was just a matter of the count of my supply. I was in fact supposed to take them only when I needed to, and even then she told me to break it in half. She said, *you make too much of the little things and you make too much of the big things.* I said, *perhaps I make too much of you.* And, *No,* she didn't think I was cultivating a goiter in my throat but that it sounded more like something hysterical. She at last called it *generalized nervous anxiety,* which is a pretty *generalized* diagnostic proposition, it seems to me. And she said it was rather like a stage fright. She said my ego was having a hard time keeping a lid on all the forces of my id, and that I had lost touch with myself, but to the degree where I would not allow myself any pleasure. I had to sort of relearn how to adjust my thought processes, but so as to resist, or renegotiate, my own innate fear structure. And I wondered if it was indeed entirely me, that is to say, I wondered if I was not somehow *clairvoyant,* if my nerves were not in fact foreboding of some great and general collapse, and I would be the barometer, then, telling, sufferingly, of crisis at large. But then I always thought one had to be a bit schizophrenic to live in New York City. I mean, yes, with all the denial that goes on. It's really something of a *split.* One is constantly bombarded by the most loathsome and degrading and indeed depressing sights, and one is constantly, but, exactly, *being put to filter them out.* And just this action of filtering them out, it in itself puts the sensibilities to insult and abuse. And I think, yes, one must be sick, or else, how does one abide? We are adaptive, yes again, but in our *adaptation* are we not, in effect, supportive? And in the name of what value do we accept, and in effect maintain, the degradation, the dishonor that bombards us every turn? Who are we protecting?

Who profits from it? Who is hiding behind it? It seems to me we have given franchise to shit.

And so too was Dawn put down with a general sense of panic and malaise, with feelings of mistrust and base inadequacy. She reached a point where all she desired was to be anaesthetized. All she desired was to be napping, or resting quietly, or else she'd cuddle up with her books and her tea, and her crayons. She was making for herself some quiet time. And, *yes,* I told her, as though to caress, *this is your shalom posture, this is your peaceful time, and this place is your hideout.*

I had the baby grand retuned for her. And I enjoyed coming home to her playing. And I would lift her in my arms, hello, and she would hug me, but as though I were the only man she had ever known. And her face would show all sorts of blush, senses of shame and modesty and confusion, and she would tear, but just a little, as though a little was all she could spare. And we could go on to kissing, and we could go on further. She was always willing to be giving of herself, and sometimes more than I felt ready to expect. But I soon realized what it was she was needing, how my just being there in her company, our simple routine. I realized it was not a lover she was needing, or else not so much as a pal, or else not so much as a standard. Together, in our sharing, and in our private ways, we were sloughing off the layers we had come to judge unsuitable. And we were smarting from our state of being raw. And she coined a term for it, she called our smarting, *Nevering.*

She thinks her mother's going through a nervous breakdown. Her very word, however, was *enjoying. Enjoying a nervous breakdown.*

—She won't leave the house, she told, on our first night in my bed. She insists on working at home. She's needed at the studio, but she's demanding everything gets routed to her at home, and she can, you know, 'cause she's the boss, so everyone's bending over backwards trying to accommodate her. I bet that's why Skye Bosch had such an attitude when she saw me in the lobby. Sometimes she takes her indignation out on me. I think she resents me. I think she's envious over that I don't do anything.

—You mean Skye isn't a messenger?

—Oh she's a messenger, all right. She works for a messenger service on Centre Street, along with all the other refugees from the halfway house. But she also works for my mother's company. She's her all-purpose gofer. And she resents having to make the extra trips.

—I figured she was just *enjoying* the convenience of working out of her home.

—My mother? There are things she has to see before she can approve them. And she's ordering they have Skye haul the stuff up and down to her. Anyway she stopped eating. And she's drinking too much coffee and she's smoking too much. She's out of control. She loses her head. You see how irritable and nasty she can be. And now she's saying maybe I should consider packing off to this boarding school somewhere. She's out of her mind. We had a fight this morning and she told me to get lost. So I'm lost.

—Yeah, but does she know *where* you're lost?

—She'll figure it out.

—Gee. I don't know, Dawn. I think you'd better call her, tell her you're here in my sleeping bag or something.

—No, Stephen. Let her figure it out. She can't cope with me just now. When she gets this way she's hopeless. I've been trained to accommodate her moods. I know when to expect to be a punching bag. This's nothing new for me. I'm just not gonna take it any more.

—How're you so sure?

—*Sure of what?*

—How are you so sure she'll figure you're here?

—Because there's no one else I care to see. She knows that. She knows how I feel about you.

—I'm confused. You kept your feelings a secret from me. My impression was that you weren't interested. That's why I more or less kept my distance.

—And because you were afraid of me?

—Because I was respecting your place.

—Do you think she's attractive?

—Who? Your mother? Of course I do. She's in excellent shape. You both are.

—She's mad about you. You're the first man she's had out to the country house. *The first that I'm aware of, anyway.* That country house is her hideout. Last summer she spent a lot of time there alone.

—And what did *you* do last summer?

—I spent a lot of time alone.

She was quiet after that. Her body was still. I thought maybe she was falling asleep. I was wishing I still had my projector, thinking how there must be some or other constellation I might liken to this temperament of hers, so cool beyond her years, and still so tender, still so vulnerable. Or else the constellation is an *aspiration,* and maybe one is being born just now.

> *So that's why He made stars,*
> *the Heavens are our scorecard!*

She rolled onto her side to face me. She was poking me with her chilly toes. *You're not sleepy at all,* I thought.

—Do you fantasize about her? she asked.

—Who?

—My mother.

I suppose I did generate one or two stock fantasies about Dorothea, but no way could I share them. I wondered if I was blushing. She was patient, but she was persistent, too. She kept on poking with the chilly toes.

—I know you do, she said, prodding me along. I have fantasies about *you*.

—Me?

I was searching the ceiling for those stars.

—One came true this afternoon, she said, and all so matter-of-factly.

—Was it nice?

—Very nice.

My eye was taken to emergent brilliance at the Scutum. . . .

It's a meteor, a fireball!

Earth's atmosphere chafes the body to an incandescence by friction. *And then another. . . .*

Fireball!

—Now it's *your* turn, she said. I know you fantasize about her.

—And how is that?

—It's obvious by how you look at her.

—How do I look at her?

—You love her ass.

—Well I'm not denying it. I just don't think I can say it.

—Then *do* it. Do it with me. Can we do it here?

—I suppose so.

—Who starts it?

—Nobody starts it. It's just going on.

—You're making love to her?

—Not exactly. Not at first.

—Give me some details. Paint a picture. What's she wearing?

—*What's she wearing?* How do you know she's not naked?

—I *don't* know. Is she?

—Actually, no. . . . She has on her black turtleneck. And her old green jodhpurs.

—Is there a riding crop in this picture?

—No. But I've seen it. She has her jodhpurs down around her ankles, and the turtleneck is pulled up over her chest. She has no panties on, no bra on. She's on her back, she's on the rug on the floor beside her bed, like she's hiding. I pass the room, the door is open. I don't see her at first but then I hear her. And I find her.

—She's masturbating.

—Her eyes are closed. She thinks she's alone. When she senses my presence she doesn't stop. My presence makes it more intense for her. She says my name and tells me to kiss her.

—Do it with me.

She kicked off the covers and slid out of her underpants. *Do it with me,* she said. I pulled up her top. *Oh, I'm gonna come, Stephen, here.*

I took her wrists and held her arms above her head. I spread her legs. *Here. . . .*

I rolled her over. She raised her hips and I pushed inside her. Then Dorothea's face entered my mind. Inside her eyes I could see how she was gone, she leaves her body and goes somewhere far away. I turned Dawn's head to see her face. She was far away. I pulled out and she dropped her hips, and I was having it, all over her backside.

I have this dream about Joey Guido. I'm with the guys and we're over his basement, and by the looks of things we've been up all night for a marathon session of poker face. We're eating fried chicken, from the Chinese take-out place, and the bucket's being tossed back and forth across the table as everybody takes turns grabbing for a piece. When we eat like this it's like a gang-rape. I'm stripping the skin off a piece of breast and thinking, this is really greasy. I was stripping the meat off the bone and dunking it in my beer. Someone says, fucking Child, you're an animal, and I think he's saying I'm a cannibal. Just then Joey Guido appears, and he's pregnant! I mean it's still our Joey Guido, it's still our Joey Jaws, only now he's pregnant! He's marching around the table with his big hands on this absurd humongous curvature of his, and I think of Atlas shouldering the vault of the heavens. And no one's saying anything, it's like no one wants to notice. I'm just about to shriek get him a cushion when everybody at the table starts hurling their skin-scraps at me. There's a pile of greasy chicken skins on my chips.

All I could think of was how good she looked, and how so out of sorts I felt.

—I'll tell you about Skye Bosch. . . .

This mood was new for Dawn, at least so far as *I* was concerned. We'd been doing gins and lime since around ten-thirty at this hangout she knew on Second Avenue. We were both pretty shit-faced. And she couldn't stop her mouth, going on about her mother and whoever she happened to recognize who was standing at the bar or coming through the doors, she was doing this association thing. We were sitting over one of those round bistro tables that really have no business in an Irish establishment but you can squeeze so many of 'em in so what the hell. I was leaning on my elbows with my face in my hands. Dawn was erect. It was nearing twelve-o'clock and she was on her second wind.

—Skye Bosch, *now get this,* used to develop photographs at the Bettmann Archive. She was a developer. She studied photography at The New School with this big time prize-winning photojournalist. He's got an odd name, it's like, *Let Chinman,* or something.

—Litt Chinitz. Yeah. He shot that *Young Negro Disciplining a Puppy.* 1962, or something. It's like anthologized all over the place. But if you really study it carefully you'll see the boy is in fact dragging the stick along the picket fence, right outta *Tom Sawyer,* and the dog looks happy as shit. *Litt Chinitz.*

—Really. So.

—*This is the gofer?*

—Yes. Wait. She was also working part-time at this film-developing factory on the West Side. That's where my mother discovered her.

—This doesn't sound like a gofer.

—I know. Wait. *It's a case of the incredible shrinking life.* My mother used to shoot on film then have them transferred onto video tape.

—Right. Now she uses video exclusively. *Which is why her pieces look like the evening news.*

—Really.

—So Skye's a photographer.

—Well, yes and no. I mean, before she got into photography, I mean, that's what my mother originally hired her for, *to shoot stills.* But it turned out she wasn't so good at it. She took too long to get into the swing of things. Everybody had to *freeze* and wait for her. She was supposed to just rush onto the set and shoot before the next camera set-up.

—Well she must have had *some* aptitude for it, or else how did she get into a class with Litt Chinitz?

—My mother says she *is* good, but that she has her own pace. *You know she's published?* Anyway, before she worked in photography at the developing, she worked in a lab at some pharmaceutical company in New Jersey. At this pharmaceutical company her job was to tend to these animals, this special batch of mice they were using in experiments for Parkinson's disease. She had to feed them, clean their cages, all these *menial* things. But she had this one special chore. It seems the mice have these two front teeth, *for all their gnawing and nibbling?*

—*Incisors.*

—Really. So these *incisors* grow continuously, and it's because they grow continuously that they have to always be gnawing and nibbling on something. *It prevents the incisors from growing right through their bottom jaws.* She had to hold the mice one by one and perform a little oral surgery.

I was preparing myself for a cringe.

—She had to trim their incisors, she continued. *And do you know how she went about this?*

—*Oh God.*

—*They had her use a nail clipper! Can you picture it, holding these little mice and clipping at their incisors!*

—Yes. *I'm afraid I can.*

—*That tops Koko's kitten!*

Gregory Vincent St. Thomasino

Der Kluge Hans

I have a weakness for the afflicted. *Or is it the affliction?* I once saw this movie, on TV one afternoon, and of all the characters the only one Dr. Frankenstein's creature would trust was this beautiful, although a little brute-looking, mute beggar girl who lives alone way up in the mountains in this cave that was, like, made by a glacier. She's a beggar girl, and she goes into the village with her bowl and bare feet begging for charity. In one scene the village bullies snatch her bowl and torment her by playing monkey in the middle with it. They laugh at her when she falls into a puddle, and none of the big burly workers standing by and looking on come to her rescue, no one, that is, except Dr. Frankenstein, who retrieves her bowl and in one remarkable moment makes eye contact with her, and in that moment they share an awareness, *an affinity,* as though to say, we're both outcasts. Her bowl, and apart from her threadbare overcoat, these are her only possessions, these and what she's been able to keep intact of herself. And you know she's, like, half naked beneath that overcoat 'cause you can see her whole white neck, and all that long and pitch-black hair. I wished if I were there, I'd be the one, I'd know her, just like Dr. Frankenstein, and I'd take my crop to those bullies and those workers. Her nose is wind-swept pink, and her hands are cold, but you know her body's warm beneath that overcoat. She's a mute-girl, and the workers shun her, they have no use for her 'cause she's afflicted, afflicted like the creature. And all men despise the wretched. It's this, I bet, can qualify every one of my relationships. I'm attracted to imperfection. It's the afflictions, what appeals to me. And I'm not so sure it's because I expect I can cure them. I'm sure it's nothing so Samaritan. I think rather it's certifiably pathological. *I found Skye Bosch attractive.*

There was something Dorothea had said about knots, something about *knots in a rope.* We encounter knots in the rope, and then the rope is somehow life itself. And we can use these knots, she said. *We can climb up these knots.*

It was well after one, now, and the sounds of the bar had grown louder, louder and clamorous. It was as though a certain violence, a violence first of clanging glasses and loud and louder voices had, at last, seized complete possession of the atmosphere. And it was almost deafeningly piercing, but like anomie with a barker's megaphone. And the place had become crowded as hell. And outside, I could see them through the windows, there were people waiting in line to come inside. I was thinking, *it'd be impossible to reach the toilet. And for Chrissake, Dawn knows these people!* All these swell and first-rate-looking guys were coming over to us, and some were making a real effort to do so, just to kneel beside her, and to gush and show off their clear skin and their bleached teeth and their clothes and their hundred-dollar haircuts. Mostly just to show off their haircuts. At one point there was four of 'em, all clustering around her and showing off their teeth, and modeling their clothes, and all kneeling, too—they had their haircuts right in our faces. *And they were really gushing.* I felt my whiskers and I thought they must think I look like a bum, or else something she just picked up off the street. Then this one guy, a real passive blanker majorette, *complaining* his good-byes and really laying it on a little thick, I thought. I thought, *this guy thinks he's in the movies, all voice and no personality. He's all voice.* He says, *tell your mother she owes me a call.* And Dawn yells back at him, *YOU call HER! I might do that,* he said. *Nice to've met you,* he said, passing his eyes over my hair. And then he lingers a spell, passing his eyes over our heads, sort of checking out the place, and he's nodding his head, as though he likes what he sees. And then he lingers a spell, passing his eyes over our heads, sort of checking out the place, and he's nodding his head, as though he likes what he sees.

—He flirts with her, she said once he was gone.

—A little crowded in here.

I was perspiring. My feet were cold and damp. When I get home, I thought, I'll change these wool socks for a cotton pair, and then I'll keep the cotton on into bed. And it occurred to me, then, that my lump had returned. But that's the way it comes on, it just sort of occurs—and *wham,* I'm under foot. And then of course I started gulping, trying to swallow as though I could swallow it away. I felt choked. The fist had put a clamp on my throat and was choking me, punishing me, murdering me. I broke a diazepam and took the half. Dawn asked, *is that wise? I have to,* I said.

All the ambient sounds of the bar, but especially the clanging of the glasses—all the voices and laughter seemed to echo and sounded dull and hollow and tinny, but as though it were coming through a cheap public address, or as though I had my ear to a wall and I were listening in. I think the odors off the grill were stimulating my digestive system. I felt this gurgling going on in my gut. Well, that really made me panic.

—*I wanna go home,* I told her. I gave her my wallet. *Pay the bill,* I said. *I'm waiting outside. I need the air.*

I think I passed out in the cab. I was vomiting in the gutter outside my building. The doorman, Mr. Nichols—*who's usually pretty shit-faced himself*—took my arm and helped us into the elevator. Dawn managed to pilot me safely to the toilet. She brought me water, and then she made a cold compress for my forehead.

—Happens to the best of 'em, she said, dabbing my eyes and the back of my neck. She helped me out of my chinos and my shirt and she brought me fresh socks and a fresh T-shirt.

—I freaked out, Dawn.

—Now I'll know to see it coming.

She tried to change my socks for me, and made an admirable attempt at it, too, but you can't really change another person's socks so I had to change 'em myself.

—Now you're home and we're alone, she said. Just allow it to pass. When the diazepam hits you're gonna fall asleep. Here, put on your bathrobe.

—Maybe it'll kill me. *Euthanasia.*

—Fat chance.

I started vomiting again, but just a little, and then just the heaving. I expected she was gonna leave the room but she stuck around and saw me through the whole damn episode. It didn't gross her out at all.

—How many did I have?

—Five or six. You hardly touched the last one.

—You know what I'm afraid of? I'm afraid it's gonna happen and I'm gonna wind up in a strait jacket at Bellevue.

—You really looked terrified. But I don't think you're the Bellevue type. You're more the Payne Whitney type.

—Then you be sure to inform the EMS of that. How do I look?

—A little pale. A little green and blue here and there. I can see your veins. *But I can always see your veins.* I don't think you look especially ghastly. Just upset. Let's just allow it to pass.

She was dabbing my face. I was leaning against the bathtub. There was something on the sleeve of my bathrobe, it looked like old snot.

I don't remember how I got into bed. It was almost ten when I opened my eyes. The place was all sunny and bright, and there was snow on the fire escape. Dawn had been up and out and back already, and every blind was open and the air was sweet with buttered toast and coffee. She heard me turn on the shower. She brought in my mug. *There's toast when you get out,* she said.

—*Coming in?*

—*I'm busy. . . .*

She was straightening up. She really did like to keep herself busy. I sat at the table in my bathrobe. She was in the kitchen, minding the toaster.

—There's more in the carafe, she said.

I filled my mug.

—This is for you, she said.

She flicked the toaster button and the toast popped up and she caught them on the plate.

—When did you learn that?

She put the plate down between us and seated herself.

—Some things you just know, she said.

She started buttering the toast. She cut them at an angle. She pushed the plate to beside my mug.

—We're invited to a party, she began. It's tonight. And I really want to go. And I don't want to go alone. *I want to go with you.*

I was dunking my toast into my coffee. I took a bite and then a sip. And then I said okay. I was thinking a party might be therapeutic. It might be therapeutic for us both.

I spent the rest of the morning reading for class. Dawn had a shower and then left to have her split-ends trimmed. In the mail there was a package from Barry in Jerusalem. In his letter he wrote how his mentor was ill and was in critical condition. *I've always known him to be generally frail and out of shape,* he wrote, *but this has hit him hard. We fear he won't pull through. There are vigils at his bedside, here at the hospital. We take our turns, myself and the three others. I'm writing this as he sleeps. We're awaiting the arrival of his son from NYC. But the man looks awful, Stephen, and when he wakes I'll have to call the nurse and leave the room so they can care for him. His wife died last year—after coming down with the same influenza! The three others—who, as you know, together with myself make up our group—were here with him at that time, and they say that since her death he's not been the same. He never really recovered from the loss. Of course our seminars have been cancelled. Hey, I came across this poem I want to tell you about. It's a sort of poem, anyway. There's this guy I used to know, but I never became too friendly with him, and I met him again a week or so ago and we started talking about things and about our families and all, and then we started talking about poetry, and he told me about how he wanted to be a poet but how life got in the way and so he couldn't really pursue it, and then he starts telling me about his little boy. So he's telling me about how his kid used to have this blanket, ever since he was an infant, it was the blanket they took him home from the hospital in. He told me how his kid used to hug it and suckle its corners and wouldn't part with it for anything. And then one day the kid starts tearing the blanket to pieces, and by that evening he'd have nothing more to do with it. Then the guy takes out his wallet, and he pulls out this piece of the blanket with a picture of his kid wrapped inside it, and he says, this is a poem. And that's it, Stephen, that's all we need to know about poetry, isn't it? But if I can find one poem in my life equal to that. . . .*

Dear Barry,

First I must say *Thank You,* my friend, for both the birthday wishes and the book. I've never heard of this *pseudonymous* Fritz Zorn, nor of this unusual book of his, *Mars.* I've never read anything quite like it. Such keenness of perception, and become so acute in his urgency! It proves, yet again, how deeply you understand our dilemma. I am up to the part where he mentions Wilhelm Reich's theory about the suppression and release of *vital energy.* Fascinating.

So sorry about Professor Levy. I do hope for his recovery. I suppose by now his son has arrived. I am concerned and I want to be kept informed.

The poem you write about is lovely. It is a love poem. I will remember it forever.

Yes, the Russell girl is here, still hiding out. I think I love her as a sister. Alas I think she is afflicted with a deep, deep loneliness. And certainly a terrible disappointment. What she needs, I think, is something to be enthusiastic about, some sort of bliss like she had with her dance. But she will never dance again, or else not the way she aspires to. Perhaps she will distinguish herself in some other way, some other artform, perhaps. I sense there is something troubling her. Some deep, deep, injury. Dawn, in all her wisdom, says I ought to learn to just allow myself to experience things, and not to analyze everything down into so many unmanageable parts. I don't stand a chance, do I?

"Que sçais je?"

From times remote there has come down a varied mass of beliefs concerning astronomical phenomena. *This is the celestial source of panic.* Signs were displayed in the heavens for the purpose of warning mankind. Eclipses, it was believed, gave expression to the distress of nature at the woes of humanity. And to the influence of the comet was ascribed such dire calamities as famine, war, floods, drought, pestilence among men and beasts, indeed the universe itself was feared to be dissolved into primeval *anomie*. Stars, though, were held to foreshow felicity.

The one key to the great enigmas of life is personality. The certain reality of the self is the starting-point of existence. Every powerful personality is a channel through which new truth comes among humanity. But alas, just as in the case of wit, personality is lost on those who have none.

For some weird reason I become all sorts of *feline* at parties. I slink around under the tables and chairs and between people's legs. Sometimes it's even noticeable. I suppose I become all weirded-out around unfamiliar people. It's something like that phantom limb phenomenon. You think you sense her near, you feel she's somehow close by and reachable and indeed you reach out to touch her, but no, she's gone. *And she really is.* Or else it's like at the bowling alley when after you've let go of the ball you still try to guide it with body language. *Go figure.*

"Stephen Agonistes"

About nine-thirty we were ready to go. I remember the time 'cause I was nervous about going. I had my brown loafers on, my nice old broken-in ones with the wheaties in the leather slots, but then Dawn said wear your rubber mocs 'cause later it might snow. I took a whole diazepam, just to round off the edges, and I didn't tell her so when I heard the blender—she was in the kitchen mixing negronis—I told her to go easy on the spirits. She said a negroni is a negroni and to keep away from straws tonight. I said the negroni is to Surrealism what cocaine is to Hip-Hop and she turned to me suspiciously and, after a pause, said *I know that.* She said we'll walk. And that's what we did.

—I don't feel I'm entirely clued-in on your dislike for Skye Bosch, I began, and in spite of how she was walking a whole half-a-storefront ahead of me. I was, and none the less, en-joying keeping an eye on her behind. She was wearing her new jeans, the old beat-up bell-bottoms that her mother paid like a thousand dollars for at Polo, the ones with the frayed slashes beneath the cheeks, the slashes so that should she bend or be, *alleluiah,* climbing a stairs her pink underpants show through. And she was wearing a bulky wool turtleneck, that she sort of strategically had tucked-in in the back. *Is there some sort of rivalry going on between you two?* I asked.

—*A rivalry?* If there is it's on her side.

She didn't bother to turn her head to answer me, she just sort of spoke at the storefronts as she *protuberated* past their displays.

—I suppose what I mean to ask is you don't seem to be too fond of each other. Did you quarrel or something? Or is it just bad chemistry?

—I think she disliked me first.

—Hey! Will you stop walking and talk to me a minute! *Thank you.* So what's the *low-down* on Skye Bosch? Why do you dislike her?

—I don't dislike her. The *low-down,* Stephen, is the girl is pixilated. *Skye Bosch thinks she sees, and, can communicate with ghosts!* You don't dislike somebody like that, you just think they're creepy.

—Well I used to be confused, *but now I'm very confused.*

—That is why my mother keeps her around, because my mother happens to be pixilated too, *or haven't you noticed. And because she believes her, and she thinks she has a gift.* So here I am, stuck with nothing more spiritually significant on my mind than to get myself pissing drunk, and having to worry over what in hell I'm going to make of my useless life, and my mother is this totally unpredictable and unreliable person who would rather sit and *chat* about ghosts with this employee of hers who refuses to just so much as look at me since I once dared to suggest that her ghost business was maybe, *just maybe, like, a metaphor? Say for like her sensitivity and need for intimacy in her life?* I don't see what she can offer you, Stephen, unless it's sex you want, and if that's the case then love is not only blind it's deaf and dumb and clips rats' teeth. Look, Stephen, I just want to have a good time. I want to smile and be happy. *I don't want to suffer.* I want to be simple and normal and have friends. *I want people to like me.* I want to buy clothes and go to concerts and parties and have boy friends. *I don't want to be deep. I don't want to read deep books. I don't care if God exists. . . .*

I let her go a whole half block before I started walking after her. I just stood there, dumfounded. At the corner she stopped, and at last turned and waited and I caught up.

—I think it's all bullshit, I told her. Everything except the sensitivity and the need for intimacy. *That stuff is for real.*

But she just stared into my face, searching my face as though she didn't hear me, or as though I had been inexcusably naive about something. It made me feel so painfully obvious.

—This is the building, she said.

Well so now I felt a panic coming on, and in spite of the negroni and in spite of the diazepam. And all sorts of ugly thoughts entered my mind. I thought that Dawn, *this dancer*—and what is dance, really, but a form of exhibitionism—I thought that she, *this dancer,* here, was probably keen on making entrances, and probably never had to deal with stage fright or with social ineptitude or with panic attacks. I felt my face was contorting to match my ugly thoughts. And how painfully obvious. How painfully obvious that I was trying to uncontort my face. I had to force myself to move, force myself to enter the building. I felt leaden, and yet my body wanted to turn and flee. And I knew I had to keep it to myself, I knew that if I told her how I felt, *what I was going through,* it would destroy whatever confidence she had left in me, if indeed there was any left.

On the elevator I told her, *you're more than a party girl.* But as the seconds passed, as I awaited her response, I was stupefied, mortified, by the impression that my opinion no longer mattered to her.

The elevator jerked itself open to our floor. Already we could hear the sound of music. *And how above the routine and repetitious-sounding bass, a just as routine and repetitious sound of voices and laughter.* I followed her to the apartment. I felt like a machine. All automatic and automaton. And I felt *obvious,* as I took my place beside her at the door. She tried the buzzer and we waited for an answer. She started shaking out her hair—but right there, in front of the apartment, as we waited for an answer to the door. She was bent over, as though to put her chin between her knees, and it was something right out of the barre, or something right out of Nadia Comaneci, for Chrissake, bobbing her head to shake out her hair. And how I wanted to fall to my knees—to entomb my face inside her perfectly proportioned bottom. *I really longed for something involuntary.* My mouth had gone all sticky and dry, my legs were totally numb. I felt like I was entering a sickroom, *and damn if I didn't catch a whiff of clove and antiseptic.*

—There's a mirror back by the elevator, I said. Why don't you use it?

—I don't need it. *Go look at your face.*

—I don't need to look at my face. *I know how I feel.* I shouldn't be here. I should be home.

—I'm sorry I said that, Stephen. I'm really sorry.

She turned to face me and pushed some hair off my forehead.

—It's not your fault, I told her. It's all me. *Everything is right, except me.*

She put her arms around me and held me. I don't think she expected me to reciprocate. I couldn't anyway, my arms were numb.

—I have a birthday surprise, she said.

—For me?

Again she tried the buzzer, and this time someone answered. But no sooner did she say *this is Stephen* to our host, Skye Bosch emerged out of the frieze. She took my arm and when I turned said *Surprise!* And then she turned me in Skye's direction. *I knew I caught a whiff of patchouli out there in the hall!*

—Hello Bosch, I managed to get out.

My tongue must be all white, I was thinking. *And that caked white stuff at the margins of my mouth.* And I wished I had taken Dawn's advice and checked my face in the mirror.

—Hello Stephen. Nice to see you.

And indeed she was pretty glad to see me. She didn't try to hide it, the way she said my name, right into my eyes. She had a drink in her hands and she was tilting it up at her chest, just so, and she was sort of poking at the wedge of lime with her stirrer. My eyes then locked onto her fingernails, which were right above her chest, but just as instantly I corrected myself. I know she was waiting for me to say something, but I felt like a mute. I wanted to motion at my mouth with my fingers, right out of Quasimodo. *Drink, drink. . . .*

—I'm having gin rickey, she said.

Somewhat retardedly I bobbed my head.

—I'll get one for you. Wait here. . . .

I looked down at my rubbers, and probably still bobbing my head I looked around to see what the other guys had on. I was the only idiot in rubbers, everyone else had real shoes on. And I still had my coat and mittens on. I looked around for Dawn, and glory be my eyes landed smack on Skye's behind as she was getting my drink. I thought, *is this too obvious?* She turned and I was smack onto her fly. I raised my eyes to her face and she was looking right at me, as though to realize I was ogling her body. But she looked happy, and totally agreeable. She handed me the gin and I think I smiled and I think I was bobbing my head as I brought it to my lips.

—Don't spill it, now.

She could see my hands were trembling. And I told myself, *this could go either way. Either I get a grip and calm myself or I make a pathetic fool of myself.*

—I like your apartment, she said.

—Thank you. Next time, perhaps, you'll get to see it all.

Well at least the drink was working. My mouth was beginning to unstick itself.

—I'm really sorry for leaving that way. I was having one of the worst days of my life.

And with that she rolled her eyes. *And there's that blue,* I told myself. Her shoulder did a little twitch.

—It's okay. How's your apartment, after the break-in and all?

—I had to put new locks on the door. And I went to the shelter and I adopted a puppy.

—You rescued a puppy? Excellent. What breed? What color?

—He's all black. Mostly Lab. They told me he was born there, in the shelter.

—So you're his first human counterpart. Do we have a name?

—Well not yet. Not exactly. I don't know if I should give him a human name or a dog name or make something up for him.

—It's a problem. I know. Like whether to name him, say, *Montague,* or, say, *Montage.* Like, *Montage* would refer to his being a bit of an edit, or a mix.

This love seat behind us got free and we sat and I sort of pushed my coat off my shoulders and let it fall behind me. She was looking at my scarf.

—Do you like this scarf? This is a black camel-hair scarf. It's pretty old. It was my father's. I'm discovering all these neat things he had.

—I think it reminds me of my puppy. So do you know who's here? Do you know Julia Kemble? Her father's running for mayor. I'm a volunteer.

—Oh wow. That's interesting. Where are you volunteering? The Bronx?

—I will be, eventually. So far I did some work in the Village, at their headquarters. But in the spring I'll be working in The Bronx. It'll be more convenient for me.

—You know, Bosch, if I were running for mayor, my entire campaign would be based upon my pledge to paint all the bridges green.

And at that point, but I confess it, I might have gone off onto one of my digressions or *discontinuities* as *Dr. P.* is wont to say, but I held on. Fortunately she didn't ask me to elaborate. And then I sort of wished I hadn't said it. But I was overheard by this trio who were standing just before us. A really swell-looking young man with a hundred-dollar haircut turned to face us and with just a bit too much brio in his voice remarked, *that's a brilliant idea! Why are all our bridges gray?* And no doubt to call attention to himself, he continued *these are institutional colors! And while, certainly, our bridges are institutions. . . .*

—They are monuments, I interjected.

He obviously did not appreciate my interrupting his performance.

—Why must we make them eyesores? he continued, nevertheless.

—It's because, I averred—*and perhaps against my better judgment, for his last was not directed to me, or to Bosch, but and somewhat discourteously I thought back to those with whom he had been standing*—a pragmatist policy—and curiously, this goes for Marxism as well—has no aesthetics. The pragmatist views aesthetics as a sort of luxury. They select their paint not according to *color,* but to cost and to budget, and to what's on hand in the shops. The aesthetic and psychological effects, if you will, of their selection, never come into play. But as though the only *green* they understand is, well.

—Julia! the young man then called across the room, interrupting me so. Julia, do you know this fellow here?

He waved his hand for her to come. I looked to Bosch and saw she was turned to see for herself.

—She's coming over, she said beneath her breath—and with something of a not too inconspicuous fret. And her shoulder was twitching. She sort of bit her bottom lip in apprehensiveness. I wondered if the others were noticing.

As Julia the would-be mayor's daughter came near, the young man sort of caught her with his arm around her waist and pointed with his drink.

—Julia, this fellow here wants to be parks commissioner.

The young woman smiled, she looked all tan and trim, and in somewise Middle Eastern. She was smiling as though about to breathe a grace upon my head, or else maybe it was the babba ghanouj on her breath.

—So long as you don't want to be mayor, she said and just as quickly turned her perfect almond eyes. Can you come in tomorrow, Skye? *We really need you.*

Poor Bosch was caught off guard.

—*Tomorrow?*

—We really need you. Say good-bye to me before you leave.

And then she left us—less so much as an adieu—to rejoin her *cluster* elsewhere. The young man—he too less so much as an adieu—left with her. I looked at Bosch and was about to execute a *par for the course-cum-go figure* sort of shrug when she rose and with a none-too-subdued huff and puff said, *I'll be right back.*

I finished off my gin as I watched her cross the room to where Julia Kemble was remaining. *After a while that twitch is really noticeable.* And I started humming this snake charmer tune, and I made this terrific segue into the theme from the movie *Exodus.* I watched her get her attention and then say something into her ear. Meanwhile I had kicked off my rubbers and was kicking them out of sight under the love seat. I brought up my feet and sort of tucked them out of sight under my coat. At last I was getting comfortable, and despite the company. The place where Bosch had been sitting was sort of out-gassing patchouli, though by now it was not entirely unpleasant. In fact I think it was beginning to appeal to me.

All the same I figured this is easily remedied, I'll just fix her up with some eau de Chanel.

I was giving the once-over to the wedge of lime at the bottom of my glass and attempting to figure why I had the craving for sweet ham and pineapple when I became aware of this conversation that was going on just to my left. They were *discoursing* on the significance of Bastille Day, and they were saying all these very *chichi* radical pseudo-leftist-cum-progressive-cum-conformist sorts of things, and I remembered what Barry had told me over burgers and fries one evening in the Village after we had seen the film of Joyce's *Ulysses* at this dumpy old art house on Bleecker Street. He had just finished *discoursing* on Allen's *Crimes and Misdemeanors,* in particular about this *binary* thing between Judah Rosenthal and Rabbi Ben, and how as Rabbi Ben goes blind the more does Judah Rosenthal go through with the murder of his mistress, and how although Rabbi Ben is going blind he can still see the difference between right and wrong and how in the end God turns a blind eye to the crimes of man or else God is unable, *or blind,* to intercede in the affairs of men but that God is only blind to the degree that man does not have faith in Him. Well anyway and then he says that what it meant to *storm the Bastille* was that in the wink of an eye all these common criminals were given the privileged status of being political and economic prisoners and that the same thing was going on in this country under the guise of civil liberties and the phenomenon of celebrity lawyers and I remembered though I cannot tell you why his also saying that since his sister's rhinoplasty she's become the perfect prude. Just then Dawn came by and sat and lifted my coat and gave a tug on my pinkie toe.

—I saw you sipping from the stirrer. What did we say about straws?

—She went easy on the gin.

—And heavy on the patchouli?

—After a while it becomes endearing. *I hope.*

—Are you all right?

—I'm all right. I'm even making myself at home, as you can see. Quite a crew you have here.

—Listen, I think I'm gonna leave for a while. Would that be okay? I'm going downstairs with a couple of friends. We might go to a bar. And then I'll come back later. Will you be okay?

I smiled and sort of bobbed my head okay. She looked around the floor for my rubbers.

—Are you sure you'll be all right here without me?

—Sure. I'm hanging out with Skye. That is as soon as she gets back. She's over there talking to Julia Kemble.

Then she gave me that searching look again, as though she didn't hear what I was saying, or as though I had been inexcusably naive about something. It made me start to feel obvious again. And it occurred to me, *her mother does that too.*

—If you want to bring her home with you, you can, she said.

—What about you?

She continued searching, only this time it was lovingly so, or maybe she was only stuck on what she felt she had to say. And *I* was sort of searching her. I was noticing, and enjoying, the color pattern of her jeans. The indigo was faded beautifully, and then symmetrically, like seasonal rings, but I mean the area around her crotch. *But as though her vulva had distressed an impression into them.* There was this crease and it was dark blue, surrounded by a lighter and then darker shades of blue. Something like Dante's *Paradiso.* And I was thinking, *that's a rose, that's a blessed rose.*

—What difference does it make? she said.

I was uncertain over how to interpret this. I thought maybe she had only failed to make the proper inflection. Anyhow, and quite involuntarily, my right eyebrow shot up.

—I'll see you in the morning, she said.

I couldn't think about what she was telling me, or what she was trying to say. It wouldn't register. It wasn't making any ready impression. It went in one ear and spilled out the other. It would have taken too much energy for me to then appreciate all the possible consequences and permutations of it all. Between the drink and the diazepam, I was at last very pleasantly polluted, and I did not feel like concentrating. But all the same my body language was answering her, and whatever it was I was saying, she took it as a sign of agreement.

She turned her face to the door where these two swell-looking guys were waiting with their coats and umbrellas and bowler hats in their hands. I was almost about to nod my head in hello but then I didn't. And I was glad I didn't because they looked a little too swell to be the sort of guys who nod hello across a room. Then she tugged on my pinkie toe again.

—I'll see you in the morning.

I suppose she was feeling guilty about leaving, about bringing me there and then leaving me alone, *but then she knew Bosch was gonna be there.* I suppose it wasn't so much her leaving with those guys as it was just the fact that she was leaving. It meant our relationship had changed, and in effect she was surrendering me to Bosch. Anyhow, so long as I was sitting there with Bosch, my whole mood had changed, and I was enjoying myself. At that moment the whole damn woolly and afflicted world could have reeled an irrecoverable tailspin, and I would be content to remain just as I was, just plopped there with all these strangers, and then for once not feeling any need to interpret myself, and then for once not feeling any panic. She left, and as soon as she was gone, Bosch returned. And she had her coat on.

—I'm getting out of here, Stephen. Walk me outside?

I had to get on my knees to fish out my rubbers. I suppose I must have looked pretty retarded—to Julia Kemble and her Ogpu gang—but I was actually enjoying myself, *prodding with my paws for my rubbers.* I found a nice old schoolbus-yellow No. 2 under there, a genuine Dixon Ticonderoga. I secretly slid it up my sleeve for a sort of unexpected söuvenïr. On the way out I waved my mitten and said *Thank you!* They ignored me, every one of them.

Well I suppose she was expecting me to say something, to ask what was up and why we left so abruptly but I still didn't feel like speaking, or even thinking, for that matter. And she was obviously keeping to herself, I mean not in any distant or un-communicative sense but she was obviously keeping to herself. I thought the elevator was running a bit unusually slowly, and it was rocking somewhat, too, and it was creaking, and when at last we reached the lobby floor the creaking stopped and this scary humming sound began. It was humming like in old model-train transformers, or like in old worn-out kitchen ap-pliances, like in worn-out blenders with the blades all seized up and sounding ready to explode, and the door wasn't opening for us. Then she kicked it with her heavy engineer's boot, and it jerked itself open.

Once outside she said she felt like walking. At first I didn't know if this meant walking alone or together but she took my arm and led the way and so I naturally, and happily, went along. Actually I was trying to imagine what she'd look like in a pair of scuffy old black penny loafers, with Mercury dimes in the leather slots. And I wanted to see her eyes, so I stopped us and I turned to face her. And there it was, opalescent, like cat's-eye. And the Sherpa bear curls on the forehead. I kissed her, just once, just a little tap on her lips, and she closed her eyes and we embraced, and then we kissed for real.

—Let's get a cab and go to my place.

—My puppy, she said. Come home with me. . . .

I held her hand in the cab. She gave the driver the address and some directions. All the roads were unfamiliar to me, I mean of course I knew the FDR Drive, but I don't think I was ever on it this far north. We drove way beyond Yankee stadium, and the road was pitch-dark 'cept for the headlights. And on the side of the road I could see old bumpers and tailpipes and hubcaps and whole quarter-panels and fragments of taillights glowing in the headlights, and all the cars were speeding by, and I thought if we break down here, forget it. And I saw, how, how now and again the gray and ferocious façade of the hollowed-out hull of apartment buildings would appear out of the darkness above us, and seem to spite down upon us, but like some spiteful dysangelist just counting its moment to strike. I started counting out the cars as they sped by, just to try to occupy my mind. I think I got to 52. I was really going on and I think I had something of a rally going when I realized she was looking at me somewhat inquisitively, so I stopped. We turned off at Fordham Road. At the intersection, waiting in the traffic for the light, these little South American Indian people were going car to car selling bouquets of flowers, and I was thinking, this is the size and the sort of people Christopher Columbus encountered. *And like for Chrissake, they were cannibals!* And as we crept up closer to the light, we saw that up ahead at the corner was a crew of black men with squeegees, *it was a squeegee posse,* and they were leaning over the windshields of the cars. And then the driver said something in Russian. And then the driver said in English, *Fuck you!* And then the driver started repeating himself in Russian, and hopping up and down and shaking his head *No!* He was having his conniptions. And then he asked, *Which way goes? Which way goes?* Bosch leaned forward and told him, *makes right, follows road! Fordham Road to Webster Avenue!* She was mimicking his broken English, right out of Boris and Natasha. When the light changed, the driver sped through the intersection. We drove along Fordham Road. The sidewalks were deserted, except for black men and little South American Indian people. And then the driver started checking out our faces in his rear-view mirror. I saw his eyes move from mine to hers and then back to mine and back to hers and then to the meter, and then to mine again and back to hers and back to the meter. I think he knew we were getting close, and maybe he was trying to determine whether we were the type who bolt without paying. And then he said, and with something of an incongruous braggadocio, *I have psychology degree! Ph.D. degree!* I took out my wallet and started counting for the fare. I got ready with two twenties and a ten. I sat back again and took Bosch's hand again. I was staring—and I think with admiration, *or else with some sort of unthought-of craving*—at the silver buckles on her black boot straps. The driver said something in Russian again, and then he switched on this boombox he had beside him on the seat. Bosch whispered to me *we're almost there.* He was having himself a fit having to keep his eyes on us and on the road and on the meter, and then on the dial for the station. And then he set it on a call-in talk show, and sort of rested his hand atop the meter. He was patting the top of the meter, and even stroking it some, but as though it were the head of his companion, or of his mascot. Maybe he talks to it in Russian, I was thinking. Maybe he blows it kisses. Or maybe he thought he could make the numbers tally faster. We could see how around his elbow there were these gross little pink blemishes, like impetigo or psoriasis or shingles or something. *Left turn here,* Bosch told him. I think by now we both felt a little sorry for him. The radio talk show host was—*but almost to a point of doing camp*—a sort of neo-retro-ultra-paleo-conservative type, it took just a second to catch on to where he was coming from, and to what he was railing against. Crime and welfare and abortion and school lunches and all sorts of political correctness, and feminists and gays and lesbians and same-sex marriages and all sorts of taxes and government spending, and the crime done by children born to unwed mothers. And then he said he was gonna do a segment he called a *gene pool update,* and he introduced it with the theme song, Love Child.

It was the air outside Bosch's building. It was foul, really foul. I mean it smelled really bad. It smelled of beer and of urine and of vomit and of decomposition. It smelled of dead animals. And of dirty feet. The driver was complaining that he didn't know his way back *onto* Manhattan. Bosch ignored him. I told him, *Sorry, I'm not from around here.* It was already close to midnight, and still the babel of children's voices, and of their mothers and their don, and then of laughing and of general carousing could be heard out of the open windows and above the salsa music in the double-parked living rooms. I followed close behind her through the vestibule, and into this desolation of a lobby. All the prewar walls were stripped bare. You could make out the spots where the mirrors used to be. Above the elevator, this ugly adhesive sign read NO SMOKING. And underneath the NO SMOKING, written in by hand in gold laundry marker, was NO FUMADERO NO. *This's the sort of building where you get burgled by your neighbor,* I thought. And I expected a Dominican version of Alex and his droogs to be lounging in wait.

—We have to take the stairs. The elevator's broken.

The pins in her new locks were sticky, she had to keep reinserting the key into the cylinder and jiggling it, and then we heard her puppy come to the door, but he wasn't barking, actually it sounded like he yawned. When at last the door was opened the dog began to hop and bob and chase his tail. She showed him his leash and he sat still and allowed her to check him and attach it. He got to his feet and put his nose right to the door.

—Let me take him for his walk. *Mi casa es su casa. . . .*

There was a motor scooter parked in her living room. It had a black messenger's pouch hanging from the handlebars. The pouch had the name and number of the messenger service written in gold laundry marker on its flap. Her helmet, and with some scary-looking scratch marks on the visor, was settled upside down on the seat. The scooter had a scratched-up decal logo of the company on its rear fender, something like the skull and crossbones. And then I noticed how the chain was dangling off its gear. I smarted some after seeing this, 'cause probably it meant she was in trouble for not being able to return it back to Centre Street, and knowing there was no way she could get it down those stairs. And I wondered just how long the elevator had been broken, and what a senseless and useless situation for her, on top of everything else she had to cope with.

The paint was peeling off the ceiling, I could see where whole peels of paint had fallen down, and there were wide areas of old water stains, all across the ceiling. I thought, I bet years ago there was a fire in the apartment upstairs. *This place hasn't been painted for decades.* Her furniture was really old, and pretty much the sort of stuff you pick up off the street. But all the same the place was clean. And I suppose the sofa looked okay, it wasn't all that shabby, or too badly stained or, like, moldy or anything, except maybe for some burn holes. And I thought, I suppose I have some shabby shirts in my drawers, shabby as in frayed at the collar. I'm terrible, left on my own like this. And another thing I do is I imagine myself at my own funeral, and I can even bring myself to tears, it's like I'm mourning the loss of myself. Or else I'm sitting at a table at the restaurant at Grand Central, and all the sounds of all the activity, and of the voices and the schedule announcements, are echoing all over, and sitting at my table are these two young women, and they're both wearing brown ribbed turtlenecks, and brown berets, and they're both wearing glasses, cherry James Joyce full moons. Very studious, very nice, I'm thinking. And then the one is mushing her nose into the ear of the other, and she starts kissing her, and petting her, and caressing her breast, and then I realize the two are, *but really,* necking right there at my table, and I'm thinking, *isn't this inappropriate?*

She had a load of books, mostly in this one pretty beat-up bookcase, but also in neat stacks piled on the floor, and then piled into these old metal milk crates. Most of them were paperbacks, and most of 'em, I could tell, were bought secondhand, and probably from street venders. Some of 'em even had the original Edward Gorey covers, these being the old Doubleday Anchors, mostly from the 50s, and the neat thing about these is sometimes you have to search the covers to find Gorey's initials. Sometimes they're hidden in the background, like in a topiary or a shrub, and sometimes they're hidden in the hem of a lady's garment, or in a bunch of roses, and sometimes they're hidden in the crosshatching, or in the wall-paper frieze. And I noticed she had kept her student textbooks, and a loose-leaf binder with the insignia of Columbia on the cover, and she also had some books on law, and a couple on tenant's rights, which would be appropriate, I figured, seeing how her landlord keeps the place. She had all the usual classics, and quite a few of these in Gorey covers. She had a great old beat-up Penguin Tolstoy's *War and Peace,* and a whole lot of contemporary stuff, mostly stuff I had either heard of or had seen advertised or had read about somewhere but hadn't felt any great compunction to take home and read, anyway they're all being made into movies. And then I saw she had some books by Jacques Lacan, and then a few by Thomas Szasz, and some by Sullivan, and some by Arieti, and then a whole mess of these dictionaries and *layman's guides* to self-analysis and psychoanalysis and general psychology. In fact the whole top shelf of the bookcase was taken up by stacks of books all to do with psychology and self-analysis, and they were stacked two deep. I removed some of the first row and found behind it all these titles by Wilhelm Reich, and then suddenly I think I went delirious, or else I almost blacked out, I felt this sudden confusion and lightheadedness, and I heard my voice utter a word and I was trying to repeat it to myself. I took a step backward and just missed the scooter. I landed on the sofa. And then I heard her key in the door, I raised my eyes and saw her stack of photography books, and I thought, *Chrissake, they even took her cameras.*

—Let me feed him, she said.

I heard her pour out some food and run the water. She called to me to remove my coat.

—You can wash your hands in the bathroom. It's this way. You have to go through the bedroom.

On my way I passed by the kitchen.

—His bowl was completely empty, she said.

—He was hungry. He's a handsome puppy.

—*Say thank you, Monty.* See how big his paws are?

—He's gonna be a big dog. *Big Monty dog.*

—Go wash your hands. . . .

When I got out she handed me a pipe and a lighter. She said stay here, meaning here in the bedroom, and closed the bathroom door behind her. Already the air was sweet, and the pipe was warm. I took one hit, and right away had to sit myself down on the bed, or else I think I would've collapsed. My shoulders and my neck, and my head, felt as though I had helium in them. I was swiveling my head and my shoulders around in circles, and I couldn't tell if I was cracking my neck. The sensation spread into my chest, into my waist and my hips and my legs. I felt as light as air. And I had to stretch my arms. I held them outstretched, like the airplane. Then I put my palms together and tried pressing them together at my chest, isometric style. I couldn't tell if I had any strength in my arms. I fell back upon the bed, and I was rolling my body over my arms, I needed the sensation of feeling pressure on my arms. I was curling up and then stretching out. I felt like a cat. I kicked off my rubbers and tucked my knees up against my chest, then I stretched out my legs as far as I could reach. I couldn't tell if I was straining myself. I was stretching out my legs and swiveling my feet in little circles, and at the same time I had my arms stretched out above my head and I was stretching out my fingers. Everywhere on my body, every muscle of my body, I felt the need to stretch and exercise. Even my eyes. I was opening and closing my eyelids, and looking wide all around me. And my lips. And my mouth. I was puckering and pouting and frowning and smiling wide and then shrinking up my entire face. And then suddenly I jerked so violently, so involuntarily, that for a moment I thought I might have snapped my neck. Little by little this spasm started up in my lower spine and it intensified into this dog shaking the wet from its fur. And my nose started running.

When I opened my eyes I was lying back on the bed. The room was dark. And I was naked. Bosch was sitting at her vanity, brushing her hair out from the nape of her neck. I watched her light a cigarette, and in the sudden illumination of the flame I saw myself in the mirror. But the way she was seated upon her bench—I could see the curve of her behind, the way her hips were just sort of plopped down on the bench. And it was absolutely archetypal. I rose and sat myself beside her. She turned to face me, lifted her leg over, and we were both sitting astride. I took the brush and very carefully pushed her bangs into place. And how they sprang, the coils, into place, as though they were alive. Even in the dark, I could see the color of her eyes. That kinesthetic Matisse blue, that would not be humbled by the dark. She took the brush from my hand and took both my hands and kissed the palms of my hands. I tried to kiss her in return, but she prevented me. She put her fingers on my lips, and she closed my eyes. She took my hands and led me to the bed. And she took hold of me. And she took me with her lips.

When I opened my eyes I found her standing beside the window. She held a glass to her lips. There was a brilliance of moonlight reflecting off the stem of the glass. I saw the glow of her cigarette. And then I noticed the glass she held was empty. She was still undressed, and now I could see her silhouette.

—What do you see out there? I asked.

—I heard voices. Like shouting. There's a fight going on. In the other building, across the courtyard.

There was a bottle on the vanity. And another glass. I rose and took the bottle and the glass with me back to the bed.

—Come. Sit with me.

I poured some wine into our glasses.

—Here's to Skye Bosch.

—And here's to Stephen Child. . . .

And just saying her name. I think, for the first time in my life, I was genuinely delighted. Actually, I felt like I was going to levitate. I still had the sensation of having helium in my veins. And I could not help but wonder if this was what Reich's release of vital energy was all about. But I could not, so impolitely, and so inappropriately, and so uncouthly, allow myself to drift away. I don't know why, perhaps it's force of habit, perhaps it's automatic, but my natural tendency is to withdraw into myself. And even now, even here, when I am in the presence of Beauty.

—Will you confide in me? she asked.

I changed my position, making myself more comfortable. She changed hers too. We were both cross-legged, now, facing each other.

—Okay, what do you want to know?

—Thea told me you see an analyst.

—Really?

—Is that all right? See we were talking and I told her I was looking for someone. I had inquired with someone and was turned down, and I was telling her how I felt about that, that I didn't know that you could be turned down.

—Was his schedule full?

—Yes. Exactly. Thea is very open about her therapy, and has a very positive opinion about analysis, and when I told her my decision she was very pleased and very happy for me. But she told me it was very common to get turned down, and that you could be turned down several times before you hook up with someone.

—That's very true. Sometimes you have to start out with a list of names and try them one by one before you finally get to see someone. When she told you I was seeing someone, did she go into any details?

—No. And I would not have asked. When she mentioned you to me, it was really in a positive spirit, it wasn't at all gossipy. It was in the best interests. She was encouraging me. Knowing Thea, if she thought you would have minded, she never would have mentioned it.

—I understand. It's okay.

But all the same, I didn't know Thea, *Dorothea,* was in analysis. All the times we discussed psychoanalysis, and with all that I had told her about myself, she never divulged a word about her being in therapy, or really anything about her personal history so far as psychoanalysis was concerned. Fact is, I came to conclude talk therapy was a bit too down to earth for Dorothea. Indeed I reckoned Dorothea was beyond talk therapy, and was onto more advanced psychology. I decided not to *divulge* this to Bosch. Not at that moment, anyway.

—So what do you want to know?

—Well I do, now, have a list of names, and I'm going to continue to call. I just wanted to know if you thought it was worth your while going. If you had any second thoughts about it. If you thought it was helping.

—It helps. . . .

I think if I could relive the scene, I think I would have played it differently, I think I would have just allowed myself to float away. Or else everything I said would have been said differently. Whenever I talk about myself I always end up hating what I say. And it's not necessarily the case that I only would have said it differently. It's really more that I just hate knowing that it all pertains to me.

—It helps a lot, I said. So far as its being worth my while, it seems to go through phases. I've been going a long time, pretty steadily all my life, so I don't know how good, or how suitable a model I can be for you. I suppose the short answer is, *yes.* I'm still alive so it must be helping.

—It helps you to cope. Right? It helps to have someone impartial to talk to. Someone, nonjudgmental.

—It goes through phases on both sides of the desk. I think, when it's really working, which is to say when you're both suitably matched, well like they say, then it's like a journey you take together.

—That's an interesting way of putting it.

—About its being impartial, or, nonjudgmental, well, like I said, it goes through phases.

—It's like, progressive.

—Yes. But there isn't any sort of schedule. Like in my case, we don't have a time-oriented goal, except to say my well-being. *Whatever that turns out to be.*

—It goes through phases. . . .

—In my case, well, it seems to me there was the *coaching phase,* and that was a period of encouragement and support. But at that time I was just a kid, and in time I came to realize that I was in fact being guided through a crisis, through a life-altering crisis. I was in a state of emergency, and funny, but, when I realized what my situation had been, when from the distance of time I saw it for what it was, and I realized that what I had taken for ordinary encouragement and support was really in fact intense, crucial therapy, therapy that helped determine my mental and emotional well-being. . . . Gee, like,

I think whereas I should have been thankful, and appreciative, instead I was overcome by feelings of resentment, and anger and indignation.

—Wow. . . . Does it hurt you to bring it all back up?

—A little. I'm not sure. Maybe it hurts a lot and I don't realize the extent, the intensity, the breadth of it all. Or maybe it doesn't hurt at all. Maybe it's a prize I've won. It's my story, and maybe I should see it as, well, it's no longer me, but it's mine, it belongs to me.

—What do you do with it? Granting that, what do you do with it?

—Well I think it depends on what *It* is, on the quality of *It*. There is a process, it's like, *turning straw into gold*. When this happened to me, that is, when I began to feel my resentment, that's when the antagonism phase started. I don't think the antagonism phase is ever really done away with. I think it's always there, like buried land mines. And sometimes you just can't resist the temptation to leap on one.

Well by this point I was totally sober, I think, and I could hear in my voice the ole calculating machine kicking in. Bosch too sensed a sort of modulation had taken place in the proceedings, but this was just what she wanted. We filled our glasses and for the next few minutes sat quietly drinking our wine. I told her I was unable to talk about it in any general or abstract terms, that it was always personal. That the best she could do was try to glean from my experience whatever she thought she could apply to her own. She got up and put on her robe. I pulled on my shorts and T-shirt. We filled our glasses and made ourselves comfortable again. The wine was at last kicking in, again, and it was fueling the machine.

—Well at this point, I continued, returning to my story, we were concentrating on my problem with distractions, or rather, *discontinuities,* as they so academically term it. You see my mind tends to wander. When I was a kid, well I guess you could say I was prone to daydreaming. But I wasn't exactly *daydreaming.* What I in fact had going on was my own special talent for creating an alternative environment, *a language-scape,* I called it. My mind, my imagination, wasn't lost in wonder, on the contrary my mind was hard at work, exercising itself, developing itself in what was the development of an articulate interiority. But be that as it may, to the adults in charge of me it seemed I was given to distraction, and prone to daydream. I wasn't exactly what you might call *withdrawn,* but I did indulge my liberty for insulating myself. And this was my *indulgence of the internal.*

And at that, and to my surprise, she smiled. And her smile was lovely. And she started to giggle. And she said in the sweetest voice, *you were talking to yourself.* She hastened to add, *you were talking in your head. You were having conversations with yourself.*

—Well, yes. I was having these interior colloquies. And these were all I had. This was all I had for myself. And I was fighting to keep it. Everything else had been taken from me. Except, *me.* This was me. No one was going to cure me of me. I was just a kid and all at the same time I was fighting to convince them that my sense of interiority was what made me me and that that was what I needed to cultivate, that that was the quintessence of my personality, that that was what had survived and what must survive, and then fighting to prevent them from curing me of it. Of course I did not have this terminology at my disposal, and it was such that my frustration was compounded. A great part of my struggle was, not only to get them to understand and to accept the legitimacy of my premise, but to enlist them in my struggle, indeed my quest, my salvation, to elucidate, to make intelligible that premise.

—You must have been a very strong-willed child.

—My frustration was overwhelming. Though they were there to help me, I had no one on my side. Always, always I was reduced to a sobbing, gasping infant.

—I wish I was there. I would have taken you away.

—Thank you. The frustration made me intense. Through my sobbing and gasping, I never let go of myself. I was that beleaguered child, but my inner sense, my inner *I* was separate from that helpless body, and all the while I was calculating, and determined, that I was right, and that I knew this one thing more than they did. And I was indeed unmistaken. In time my assertions were admitted to be legitimate. Or at least immovable. I was a curiosity. I became a curiosity. And as such I was safe. In fact I was like a safe that needed to be cracked. The contents of the safe needed to be gotten to. But so that they could know the contents of my colloquies, so that this could be made available to them, and made useful to them, while preserving the integrity of my personality. So what became of all this? What tactic, what strategy did they apply? I'll tell you. We played games. Games to lower my guard and lure me out. I made lists! I became an idiot savant of lists!

—Lists. . . . That's interesting.

—Wanna know what my first list was? It was a list of all my toys!

—A list of all your toys. . . .

—I made lists of everything. Of all my clothes. Of what I saw at the park. I made lists of all the people I knew. And then for every name on the list I had to explain my relationship to that person. And what I thought about that person. And indeed like if I liked them or didn't like them, and why. My estimations of all these people, my opinions and judgments, were remarkably astute. I was shrewd and sharp and incisive. I was way in advance of my years. I was more than precocious, I was dangerous. I was already a psychologist! And I could argue. And I could defend myself. And I could penetrate the veneer of arrogance and imperiousness. And if someone didn't like me, it was because they knew I knew them, and I knew them to be false, or spiteful and malicious. But there were also people I loved on that list, and it was based on information in part derived from my list that they placed me with my Aunt Gloria.

—That's astonishing, Stephen. Do you still make lists?

—Oh boy, am I an idiot savant of lists.

—May I sample a list?

Marlon Brando's godfather
Louis Armstrong's singing voice
Leonard Bernstein's face
Bettie Page
Mother Teresa
The James Bond theme
The separation of the saucer section in Star Trek
Jerry Lewis's run
Diane Keaton doing Streetcar in Sleeper
Peter Cushing

I could have gone on interminably, and being as I have so many lists memorized, but I thought it wise to end it there, with just a sample. She was looking at me a little inquisitively. And then she asked, *How does the Louis Armstrong go?*

—I can't. I'm afraid my Louis Armstrong sounds like Tom Waits.

—I mean. . . .

She rolled her eyes, real wide. She snapped her head as though to restart her senses. *I have that effect on people.*

—I mean, she continued, you just *think* about it?

—Yes. I hear it in my head. Or else as in the case of Jerry Lewis's run, I see him doing it.

—And how about the Marlon Brando?

—For that one I need to place the sugar packets in my jowls.

—You really do have a problem, you know.

—I know. *It's an affliction. . . .*

She sort of tilted her head and said *that's astonishing, Stephen.*

—Tell me something, Bosch, I started. Did Thea offer to give you a referral? I mean, did she offer to try to get you in to see her analyst?

—No.

—That's interesting.

—It didn't occur to me to ask her. Why's that interesting?

—I don't know, it just gives me pause for thought.

—So tell me, Stephen. What's going on with Dawn? I heard she moved in with you? You came to Julia's with her and then she left with those two Wall Street types.

—I'm not officially living with Dawn. She just needed to hide out for a while. To get away from her mother. My place was convenient, that's all.

And at that moment I wished I had a telescope, or else maybe my projector going, 'cause there was so much going on on that ceiling. Each time I looked up I was witnessing to whole constellations being born. *It was a very busy night so far as the collective unconscious was concerned.* I saw their brilliances, little brilliances irrupting into being. And there were flashes—fireballs and streaks of brilliance taking aim and disappearing out of sight into the corners.

—I like your name, I said. *I certainly do.* Isn't *Skye* an island?

And was that a little delayed-action twitch I just saw?

—Dawn was told by her dance instructor that her ass was too big for the kind of dance she wants to do, she started, and with some reticence, but as though she were unsure or undecided about where she was heading. Did she tell you about that?

—No. Not about that. *Chrissake.* But I think Dawn's dance instructor is an ass for saying that. Do you know about her injury?

—It happened right after he said it. He really discouraged her. He threw her off her entire equilibrium.

—What a humiliating thing to say! Was it in front of other people?

—The entire class. He's this utterly self-absorbed middle-aged gay man, and he thinks that because he's so *affected* it gives him the right to be unsubtle. Thea told me all about him. Did you know she had a fight with him? *She went up there and punched him in his face.* And do you know about Dawn's father? *You don't know that he committed suicide?*

—That's very nice. No, I don't know anything about it.

And I didn't have time to digest it. She continued right on telling.

—He took an overdose of painkillers. Do you, uh.

And when she speaks the *uh* part she has both sets of fingers on her glass, as though to offset the twitch, which is coming across loud and clear, it's resonating down her arms and causing her wine to undulate.

—Do you know their house in Sneden's Landing? she asked.

I said yes but thought it best not to elaborate. I didn't want to say anything that might disconcert her or otherwise interrupt her telling. And I didn't want her to associate me with Dorothea any more than was officially necessary.

—He was there with Dawn, she continued. Just the two of them. It was Christmas Eve. Thea was still downtown, working all night at the studio, and when she got there Christmas morning she found Dawn waiting for her in the driveway. She had gone in to wake him, and she found his body and she ran out of the house. She was afraid to go back inside.

At first it was just some story, some horror show about some people I just happened to know. And then it hit me. *My God. That's just awful. This is unthinkable.* And she was watching me, and by my reaction it was clear to her, I really had no idea.

—*Killing himself alone with his daughter,* I said. *My God. He must have really hated them.*

—What makes you say he hated them?

—To give them *that?* No one, no one is in so much pain that he would cause his loved ones an experience like that. The sheer *grief* of it. *My God.* Was he ill? *Was he dying of something?*

—No. He was depressed.

—Good grief! And that's what he leaves his family? A suicide? *On Christmas morning, for Chrissake?*

So that was it. That must have been Dorothea's turning point. *Her real turning point.* That was the shock that drove her into oblivion. And that's why Dawn's so maladjusted. The poor bastard had failed in perfecting himself. He chose death instead of his own will to overcome himself. He chose to be reborn through death!

I wasn't sure of how upset I was, or of exactly *why* I was upset, except at the sheer thought of a man's suicide. There was this subtext to the story, something I should have figured out by now or that maybe I was trying to avoid.

—I still don't know why you say he hated them.

—Maybe *hated* is too strong a word. I did not know this man and I know nothing about what was going on between them. It's just, I think if you're not already dying from some incurable disease, no matter how much pain you're suffering otherwise, no matter how afflicted you are, I think killing yourself is always a statement, and about your family as much as about yourself or your suffering. Suicide is a statement. He was saying something.

—No, Stephen, actually I agree with you. I think he did hate his wife. But I don't understand why he did it that way. Why he did that to Dawn.

—Except maybe if he meant the pain for Thea, knowing Thea would have to live with knowing the pain and fright Dawn suffered, and have to live with knowing she could never get him back for doing that to her child.

—Wow. . . .

—Who told you all this?

—Thea told me. I thought you knew. I thought you knew all about them. Please, my telling you of this is in no way meant to be malicious.

—Of course not. Of course not.

—I just wanted to talk about it. I tried to be Dawn's friend, but as soon as I got close to her, she changed. She changed into this seriously unhappy person. But where does it all come from? Why do we act this way?

—It comes from hell. The cosmic mumbo jumbo.

I've always had a sneaking suspicion that hell was in fact nothing more than chaos, *the cosmic mumbo jumbo,* the collective *anomie* before man had realized his power to control with reason and articulation. And all his interpretation, and all his meaning and value were in fact his way of holding off, of forestalling, a reflux of hell. In his primal state, man was not a noble savage, but a wanderer in the wilderness, a sleepwalker, a sort of madman drunk on bodily influences. Insanity, lunacy, *chaos,* these are all synonymous with hell.

—So. You have to work tomorrow?

—I'm afraid so.

—And then you have to do your volunteer work?

—No. No more. I told Julia I can't come in any more.

—Really? So, like, maybe I can see you tomorrow, like for lunch?

She smiled and shook her bangs.

—You are so adorable, Bosch. I thought so since the moment I saw you. It's just so utterly incongruous to be looking at you and to be thinking of all that stuff. I don't associate you with any of that horror, and I don't want you to associate me with it, either. Okay?

She smiled and shook her bangs.

—Are you really a poet? she asked. *That's one of the things Thea told me about you.*

I pointed to my pants, she hopped up and got them from the floor beside the bed. I took my wallet from the pocket, and then this piece of paper I had tucked inside the wallet. I gave it to her to unfold.

I remember, we shared the pipe again. And I remember removing her robe. It was pretty early when I awoke, a little after five. I always awaken early when I'm not in my own bed. At some time during the night Monty had come onto the bed, and now he was poised to come onto my chest. I patted my chest for him to come, and he did, and he was, I think, rather heavy for his size. *You do have big paws,* I told him. *I'm gonna be a big dog,* he said.

That night I had the pig dream. Dorothea was a wee white piglet, with a pink corkscrew tail, and she's rolling around all invertedlike on my rug. I kneel beside her, and I take her, and I sit her up, and she pees on my rug.

About seven, while Bosch was getting dressed, I phoned a car service and arranged for a station wagon to pick us up and take us into Manhattan. When the car arrived I grabbed ahold of the scooter and without giving it a second thought carried the damn thing down the stairs and threw it into the back. I told her how nice if she would quit the messenger service, and if they gave her a hard time over the scooter or over what they owed her just to let it be and walk away from the situation. Just tell them to call it even, I told her. Her work day began at the production company studio, which was on West Houston, and after dropping her off at Centre Street she would make her way there alone. We were later going to meet for lunch at Childs, a restaurant she suggested at Fifth Avenue and 56th Street. I told her I wanted her to move in with me and to quit working for Dorothea. She could leave behind her whole past, I told her, just bring the dog, the books, and the pipe. From Centre Street I had the driver take me home. I figured I had just enough time to tell Dawn to go back home and to shower and to make it to Bloomingdale's to pick up some Chanel, and then to make it over to the restaurant.

When I reached my lobby Mr. Nichols raised his hand and tapped his visor, this is a signal he uses whenever he has information for a resident. His face had on one of those classic expressions of *there's trouble waiting upstairs.* He said that woman he's seen me with had just arrived, about ten minutes ago, and she was waiting upstairs in my apartment.

—What about the girl, the little redhead? I asked.

—No, no, no. *Just the woman.*

When I reached my door I found it was unlocked. Dorothea's pack was on the floor in my living room. Next to it were some books I had borrowed from her, and from their arrangement they looked as though they had been thrown there. A few feet farther on, and towards my bedroom, was a pile of clothes belonging to Dawn. And then I heard dresser drawers opening and closing in my bedroom. She must have heard me coming in, but the sound of the dresser drawers kept on coming. I knocked on the bedroom door to get her attention.

—What's going on?

She looked really bad, and as though she had been going without sleep. Her hair was uncombed, just held off her face with a hair band. I could see her face was pale, and she looked older than usual. But she kept right on going through my drawers.

—Can I help you? I said. And then I lost it a little. *What the fuck's going on, Dorothea?*

She wouldn't turn to face me.

—You were supposed to be with Dawn last night.

I didn't know how to answer. I could hear the stress in her voice.

—Did you go to a party with my daughter last night?

—Yes.

She still wouldn't turn to face me.

—Julia Kemble told me you left with Skye Bosch. You left without my daughter.

—Please don't mess up my clothes like that.

She was beginning to get out of hand. She was literally ransacking my drawers.

—Dorothea! Stop it! Tell me what's going on!

I was still outside the room, sort of standing in the doorway. I was afraid to go inside to stop her. Then she picked up Dawn's suitcase from the floor and opened it on the bed. I saw it was already pretty filled.

—It looks like you have it all, I said. Dorothea, please, *what's going on?*

—You went to a party with my daughter last night and you left without her.

—That's not exactly how it happened. She left first. *But so what?*

—Julia Kemble told me you left with Skye.

—Yes, but that's only after Dawn left first.

—Why did you let her leave!

She closed the suitcase and took it and started coming towards me.

—I didn't exactly *let* her leave. She left because she wanted to.

I stepped aside to let her by but she stopped right in my face. I stepped back to back away from her, but she followed right upon me, backing me into the living room.

—What's the matter? I said. *What's going on?*

—*You let my daughter leave with those barbarians!*

—What barbarians? She was going to a bar.

Then she pushed me with the suitcase.

—Get a grip, Dorothea. *What's your problem!*

Then she dropped the suitcase and grabbed me by my coat.

—*Those fucking barbarians beat up my daughter! They drugged her. They tied her up and took turns fucking her. And then they left her on the street, and they went to work!*

She made a grab for my throat. I was able to back away. Then she reached again and got me. She had me by my throat and was trying to choke me. I reached for an object, anything I could get hold of, and took hold of a book—my Idries Shah's *Wisdom of the Idiots,* in hardcover no less—and smacked her

one, one good one on her head with it spinewise. She released
me and stumbled backwards.

—*Get a fucking grip, Dorothea. Why take it out on me?*

She came at me again, and I hit her. I caught her real
good this time, right on her forehead, right between her eyes.
She stumbled again, falling backwards onto my sofa. I didn't
hit her hard enough to make her lose consciousness, but I did
make her come to her senses.

—So all this time I've known you you're really a fucking
maniac.

I think she was seeing stars. Her eyes were like rolling
around at the ceiling and her tongue was lolling at the corner
of her mouth. She had some spittle on her chin and she wiped
it away with the back of her hand, real roadhouse bar-fightlike.
Then she uttered, *you hit me, Stephen.*

—I don't know anything about what happened last night,
I said. She left because she wanted to. We went out together
but then we split up.

She said, *you don't know anything,* and got up on her feet
and gathered the books into her pack. She took the suitcase
and was making for the door.

—May I have my keys, I said.

—They're on the bed, she said, not turning around but
turning enough to see my hands. *I thought she'd be all right
with you,* she said. *That's all I wanted.* And then she turned her
shoulder and was gone.

I locked the door. I poured a glass of water and returned to
the bedroom. I saw my keys on the bed and sat myself on the
windowsill. I was trying to catch my breath. I was just beginning to realize how out of breath I was, and how terrified I was.

And how I was trembling. I was looking around to see if she had taken any of my belongings by mistake. I didn't even know what I was looking for, what I was expecting to find missing. And I was trying to figure why I didn't feel any great sense of loss, or of shame, or of guilt, for that matter, over what had just gone on, and over what had happened to Dawn. I thought maybe I was in shock. And I thought I ought to shower now, to try to calm down, and so that I can make it to Bloomingdale's.

Just the idea of Bloomingdale's, or of just getting myself outside and walking, gave me a sense of relief. But then, just as quickly, I felt my body weaken and my patience degenerate. *This was not my episode,* I told myself. *Why did I have to bear witness to this?* And then the thought entered my mind, the contempt-ible, horrible thought of Dawn and her father alone together. I tried to resist it, to resist the sound and the images that brought them before me, but I could see them, and again and again in the habit that brought them together. And I could hear Dawn's voice, forming the words against my will. *We don't come here too often in the winter, just to flush the toilets. And to play with our shit.*

And here's my body saying low and abject and contempt-ible, and my mind is saying wash your hands, wash your face, wash your body.

I ran the bath. I was soaking and imagining myself at the Chanel counter, and I was thinking about what to wear. And I was thinking about her eyes, about her eyes and the blue in *Icarus* from *Jazz,* and how such blue can make a painter mad.

Bloomingdale's is just a five- or ten-minute walk from my building, depending on the hour, and on the weather, and depending, of course, on the shoes. I was on Lexington, across the street opposite the revolving Art Deco doors. I was thinking about how great my coat felt on my body. It really fit me well. And it really kept me warm. It was just a little worn around the buttonholes. And around the collar, I suppose. I suppose I've had it for, well, going on, like, four whole years. And I was whistling the theme to the movie *The Vikings,* and making this great segue into the theme from the movie *Star Trek,* and then back into *The Vikings,* and then a segue into the Slinky song. My cousin used to have a Slinky. The Slinky is the most stupid toy in the world but it has a great theme song, right up there with *Mystery Date.* I can also do the Casper the Friendly Ghost song, and from there segue into the theme from the movie *Peyton Place.* I like the game *photography,* it's very nineteen-forties. You get a bunch of guys and gals together, you turn off the lights, *and you see what develops.* I once watched that whole stupid movie with my Aunt Gloria, and she was, like, transfixed, literally transfixed as though what the hell she was watching. And I was getting into this stare. I had this stare thing going. I had my eyes wide open. And it was tempting, almost overwhelmingly so, to just let myself go, to lose myself in my stare. I was watching the shoppers come and go, in and out, all sorts of people. People from all over the world. And thinking yes, for sure, the most beautiful women in the world can be found at Bloomingdale's. I could see myself, entering the store, in my reflection on the glass of the revolving door, and then immediately, to be wafted in the scents of the perfumes on the midway. I was bumped into by this woman. She was rushing out. She seemed as though she was fleeing a fire. Her eyes were open wide, and rather bulging and glassy, but not as though she had been crying, I mean as though she had just wakened from a terror. Could be she just had perfume in her eyes. And she had a little girl in tow. Somehow or other I caught the child's eye and she winked at me and sort of flipped her little hip at me. She was wearing these little white cowboy boots and her dress came to just below her bottom. The woman tugged on the child's arm. The child's feet were put in motion so fast, but as though they had lost contact with the floor. And then I noticed there were firefighters everywhere. Some had stationed themselves in the aisles, and some were moving about in what seemed to be a pretty well rehearsed choreography. But then I saw these were not real firefighters, these were female models made up in firefighters' uniforms. They had the black firefighter coats on, with the yellow reflective stripes, and they wore the firefighter helmets, and at the bottom just their perfect legs, and then a four-inch stiletto heel in fire-engine red, and then a wrinkle in fire-engine red ran up the back of their stockings, and in one hand they held a gleaming new red hatchet, and in the other a sample of Engine Co. No. 44 lipstick. And they all had fake mustaches in their noses, but to accentuate their Engine Co. No. 44 lips. And up and down the aisles was rolled out these flat mock-ups of fire hoses. And there were hydrants, in fire-engine red, set beside the firefighters stationed in the aisles. And then above us, suspended from the ceiling, there were tightrope walkers, made up as bellhops, and trapeze artists flipping through the air. Trapeze artists, made up as bellhops, doing flips and acrobatic stunts. There were contortionists. These slender Oriental women, made up as bellhops, and in the most discourteous of positions, going about on their hands herky-jerkylike all up and down the aisles. And as they went about they were farting perfume in blue puffs of combustion. I felt something tugging at my coat sleeve. I looked down and I saw that little girl again. She was trying to tell me something.

Cou-cou-could you co-come with mm-mme over here, over here, pu-pu. She led me by my sleeve through the counters and the crowds, to a place the other side of the midway. Her mother showed up and took her by the arm. This time she lifted the child in her arms and carried her away. The child winked at me, over her mother's shoulder, and pointed to a class of kindergartners seated on the floor. They were being addressed by a model, made up in trench coat and dark fedora hat. The fedora had a dramatic pinch to it and her eyes were concealed beneath its brim. Her belt was cinched so tightly, but to accentuate her tiny waist. She held a bottle of perfume in her hands, and she was fondling its plastic seal, as though she were about to rip it open. And she was teaching them, in a lisping Castilian voice, to say the perfume's name. *Espy.* A little boy hopped up and faced me. He said his name and held his finger to his chest. *I'm Christopher!* I felt my legs buckle out beneath me, and my backside bump against the floor. I tried to pick myself up but my legs were paralyzed. The little boy came and stood beside me. *I'm Christopher.* I know, I said. How did you get here? The little voice came against my ear, and as he did I took his hand. *Hit and run.* I shook off his hand and tried to crawl away. My legs stuck out as though they were on backwards. *Look over there.* He pointed to a woman behind the Chanel counter. *That's my friend.* But I can't see, I said. I can't see above the counter. I tried to push myself up. *She's my friend.* Yes, and I want to see her, I said. Oh help me to see. I pulled my body toward the counter. *She's my friend, and I love her.* Oh yes, I'd love to see your friend, I said. Oh please help me to see. *She's my friend.* But where is she going? Christopher, I want to see her. At last the model ripped the seal, and all the children purred and rose to their feet. Some stood on tiptoe, as though to lift their noses to the scent. The Oriental contortionists had surrounded me, their upside-down faces made expressions of curiosity to one another. It seemed to them by the way that I was holding myself up that I was trying to outdo them, and they began laughing at me, and farting perfume in my face. I reached for the child's legs and climbed up his body 'til I had him in my arms. I could taste his golden hair in my face. I managed off my knees and I lifted him, and I hurried him away to the revolving doors.

I hurried along 59th Street, and then at Fifth I turned south for the restaurant. I continued for 56th Street, but so far I could see no sign for Childs restaurant. I crossed Fifth and checked the corners, and I checked up and down the blocks, but I could find no sign for Childs restaurant. I asked a policeman but he had no idea. I asked in Tiffany, but the salesman said no, but then an older salesman had overheard my question, he took me outside to the sidewalk, he pointed to a building and said it was the corner but that Childs no longer existed. *You're too late.* But that can't be, I said. I have a date to meet there now.

I was famished. My energy, my strength was gone. I aimed myself in the direction of home.

I looked for Mr. Nichols in the lobby. I knew he'd be out getting his lunch. The building super was standing at his station. *Any women call for me,* I asked. *A little brunette with curly bangs? How about a little redhead? How about a tall blonde? No?*

When I got to my door I pushed it to see if it was unlocked. When it's not locked all the way it makes a jiggle. Anyway I wanted to startle anyone who might be waiting for me inside.

I didn't even take my coat off, I floated straight into the bedroom and sat myself on the windowsill. The drawers were still open, and my clothes were still all pushed around. Even the items on top of my dresser had been handled and pushed around and left in disarray. The closet doors were open, but aside from that, everything inside looked untouched, except that Dawn's shoes and suitcase were gone. I took the Chanel out of my pocket and tossed it onto the bed. I wished it were a bottle of gin. And then I thought of the vodka in my freezer. And I imagined myself getting up and going to it and fixing myself a drink. I knew the pear brandy would still be in the cupboard. I knew Dorothea would not have thought to look there, except maybe if she thought to retrieve Dawn's vitamins. Then the buzzer sounded, and my ears pricked up in that vestigial, involuntary way, but as though I had sensed a predator, and I thought for a moment what to do.

It sounded again. And then a series of knocks. But familiar knocks, somehow. Knocks as though to say *I'm here, I'm at the door, I'm not downstairs in the lobby.*

I felt myself start to tremble, with fear, with cold, with excitement. I couldn't feel my legs, as I made it to the door to let her in. And immediately, my stomach went into convulsions. And were it not that I had nothing inside me, I would have vomited all over her loafers, and the Mercury dimes in the slots.

—Nothing personal, I managed to get out.

—Or were you expecting me?

—Not unless you're the Grim Reaper. *Are you?*

—Never can tell.

—*Not these days.*

—Are you okay?

—I was just enjoying myself a little episode. I think I'll recover. Mind if I just sort of crash onto the sofa here.

She tried to take my arm but I somehow politely let her know I had to make it on my own. She helped me with my coat, how underneath I was wet from perspiring.

—Will you be all right?

—Yes. I'm beginning to recover. Well this is a surprise.

—I was at Bloomingdale's, she began. Just wandering around, and minding my own business, thank you, when of all things I happened to spot you at the Chanel counter. And then I see you make this beeline for the street. I didn't like the way you looked. I was worried. So I thought I'd catch up to you outside and say hello and maybe ask what was the matter. But you hurried on your way up 59th. And I just felt I had to follow you. All the way to Fifth Avenue. I guess seeing you, just seeing you, I felt I couldn't let you go.

And she began to cry. She was weeping. And I thought, *wow, that's some weeping there.*

—I couldn't let you go, she said. I lay awake at night thinking what I've done. How much I miss you. And then seeing you. Just by chance, like that. I felt, not without at least letting you know. If I made you lonely, I'm sorry.

I helped her with her coat. I wiped the bridge of my nose on her shirt sleeve, which was just my way of letting her know I was still all right with her.

—I saw you go into Tiffany, she said. And I was going to follow you inside but you came right out and then seemed to be heading home. So I followed you. I sat downstairs a few minutes, hoping you were alone, and thinking oh my God he has the Chanel, he must be up there with someone. And then the super came over and I asked him if he knew if you were alone, and he said he thought so. I asked him not to call. And then I came up. Are you hung over or something? You look like you slept on a cardboard box last night.

—I'll tell you all about it later. I'm just famished. Did you eat? Would you join me for some Ding Dong Wok?

—Why don't you shower. Put your pajamas on. I'll call.

—You know you left a coat in my closet, I called out to her from the shower. You forgot your coat. Sure you didn't just come back for your coat?

—I didn't forget my coat. I left it here. *There's a difference.* When I came out I found her in the bedroom.

—Everything all right, here? she asked. You sure it's all right?

—I can't explain this yet. I wouldn't know where to begin. Except to say, this morning, I experienced the conclusion to a totally unwieldy situation.

—You don't say. Me too.

—Let me guess. *Herr Professor Doktor Freud.*

—Remarkable. I always said you were physic.

—Well you look none the worse. What was *his* problem?

—His problem? The man was totally, but grossly, obsessed with you. He couldn't get you off his mind. He asked about you constantly. And he kept on referring to you as, *the Wunderkind.* Even after I finally got myself to stop talking about you, he kept on bringing you up. And he never really believed I wasn't still sleeping with you.

—Oh yeah? You were sleeping with him?

—Some. I couldn't get used to his body. *Or to his style.* He had this inhibition about touching himself. It really made me lonely.

—Remarkable. Say, would you receive the delivery? *I think I might need to vomit again.*

We ate. We didn't really talk. We made tea and took our cups into the bedroom. She helped me fold my clothes and put my drawers back in order. We stripped the bed and put a fresh set of sheets on, and we wound up taking out the vacuum cleaner and going over the whole damn apartment. She took off her dress and put on one of my big oxfords. It was reassuring, to say the least, to see her bottom curtsying out from beneath my long shirt again. And her legs, and especially behind her knees, and her ankle-socks and her loafers.

She helped me rearranged a load of books I'd been meaning to tend to. They were among my father's and like the history books they were useful to me now and I needed to make them more convenient. Along the way we uncovered some of my children's books. I took them into the bedroom and propped them up on top of my dresser. That's where they used to be. And I found I still had my old book ends, we found this pair of bronze busts of Abraham Lincoln, and not only were they book ends, they were a pair of banks, and they were both filled with Indian-head pennies. I put them back into service, and right where I could see them.

I sat at my desk and I gave it the once-over, and I felt it was so neat to have this desk. And all the possibilities, all the possible beginnings, all the prospects this desk now symbolized for me, as now I wanted nothing more than to put my words, my language-scape, down on paper. And I had this flash, this sudden intimation of a sense of freedom, a sense of freedom that was synonymous with possibilities. And I thought, how life is synonymous with possibilities. And I knew, that's where I'm to begin.

—I have a load of preparation to do for tomorrow, she said. I think I'll get right to work.

—I have work to do too, I said.

I watched her change back into her dress.

—I'll call, all right? After classes. Wanna see a movie?

—Sure.

—Then it's my treat, she said.

And going through the door she said stay put. I will, I said.

"Six Comets Are Coming"

I brought some books into bed with me. I was exhausted and thought maybe I'd read myself to sleep. Through my window I could see, but just above this tip of black water tower, and above the towers of the bridge, I could see the first star of the evening. I reached for the lamp, so that I could see better in the dark, and noticed my notebook there beside my bed. It was weeks since I last opened it. I took it up and held it on my chest. I had no desire to open it, just holding it and knowing it again, and knowing all the stuff I had inside it, was enough.

I reached for the lamp. And then I thought about that star again. The first star of the evening. I thought I might go up to the roof, to have a better look. I took the elevator up to the penthouse, and then the stairs to the door to the roof. And when I opened the door, I found that star again, but it was just a little *winking* star, and high in the east beyond the towers of the bridge. And all the stars I had ever known, all the stars I had never been shown how to follow, all the stars were awakened and aplay in the sky high above my building, but as though they had been waiting for me, and as though they now were welcoming me.

The wind was blowing open my robe, and causing me to tremble. And I was marching, marching in place, marching to keep myself from trembling. I was marching and *ta*-tapping on the drum I had strapped around my waist. I was marching and *ta*-tapping, reaching high my drumsticks and *ca*-clicking my drumsticks high above my head.

Embrace me!

I sang, up and up to the stars high above my head.

Take me for Your starry anatomy!

Reaching high my drumsticks, *ca*-clicking my drumsticks high above my head.

Take me for Your starry anatomy!

I was marching on the up-turned soil. I was twirling and kicking up the up-turned soil.

Oh su-sudden joy!

Take me for Your starry anatomy!

Well the story goes that I slipped and fell off the roof that night, and that I landed in the garden of the penthouse below, and with nary a scratch. I suppose that's how it happened, but I remember it differently. I didn't see God that night, but I did bear witness to a whole new constellation being born. At first I thought it was another set of twins, but then I thought, it couldn't be. There were two of them, and the one was greater than the other. I couldn't recognize their faces, or why the one seemed to be standing in protection of the other, but they seemed somehow familiar to me. And then I realized, it was a man and a woman. And then I realized there was a third. He was represented by a single star, a single *winking* star, and just at the space where the woman's womb would be

About the Author

Gregory Vincent St. Thomasino was born in Greenwich Village, New York, and was raised in both the city and in the country across the Hudson River in New Jersey. He was educated at home, eventually to enter Fordham University where he received a degree in philosophy. In 2009 he received the Distinguished Scholar Award from the Doctor of Arts in Leadership program at Franklin Pierce University in New Hampshire. He lives in Brooklyn Heights, New York, where he works as a private docent.